Black Ice Matter

Black Ice Matter

Gina Cole

First published in 2016 by Huia Publishers
39 Pipitea Street, PO Box 12280
Wellington, Aotearoa New Zealand
www.huia.co.nz

Reprinted in 2022

ISBN 978-1-77550-298-2

Copyright © Gina Cole 2016

Front cover images:
cord and characters © Gina Cole
hands © haveseen/Shutterstock.com
fire © Igor Lepilin/Unsplash.com

Back cover image:
iceberg © Tim UR/Shutterstock.com

This book is copyright. Apart from fair dealing for the purpose of private study, research, criticism or review, as permitted under the Copyright Act, no part may be reproduced by any process without the prior permission of the publisher.

A catalogue record for this book is available from the National Library of New Zealand.

In memory of Bart, my black and white

Contents

Tabua	1
Swim Bike Run	17
Till	33
Pigeon Shoot	47
Rabbit Shoot	63
Baby Doll	81
Ice	87
Grain Stacks	105
Home Detention	119
Glacier	141
Black Ice	151
0.001	163
Melt	175
Acknowledgements	189

Tabua

Serafina lay dying. She caught sight of a young Fijian man from her second-storey bedroom window, digging in the yard next door of Kerpal the Indian taxi driver. He stopped digging, leaned on his shovel, and looked up towards her window. The late afternoon cacophony had begun. Endless jazz licks, barking dogs, buses changing gear, car horns, high-pitched laughter, fireworks and the rolling intonations of deep-voiced Fijians.

Why did he stare at her? Had he paused for a break? From her vantage point, it looked as though he was working on something important for Kerpal, not just ordinary yard work clearing the leaves of the breadfruit tree. She had seen this type of work before when her cousins cleared a site to install a scaffolding structure for a funeral or some such gathering. Typical! Instead of working, he stood like a carving in the middle of the yard leaning on his shovel. He suffered from the national malaise. No wonder nothing ever gets done in this country, she thought. How could anything ever get done with everyone standing around leaning on shovels, or sitting around kava bowls brooding, or loafing on the Suva roadsides as the road workers did, gathered around dusty orange cones?

She had seen how the road workers would labour for weeks filling in cavernous potholes around Suva city. The weather and the regime always thwarted their efforts. They had no equipment to prepare the potholes. No tamper machines to compact the fill. In desperation, they would throw hot black asphalt into a pothole and run a truck tyre over it once. They left the new asphalt jagged around the edges and dipped in the middle, and the next downpour of pounding Suva rain would grind out the black sticky mixture and wash it to the side of the road, leaving the potholes bigger than ever. She would bet money the road workers knew the pointlessness of their efforts. They made a great show of trying to fix the potholes anyway, and everyone suffered the consequences of their shoddy work. They made sure to look the part; to do something, anything, even if it was only standing around leaning on their shovels, before moving on to the next pothole, dragging their feet like a herd of disconsolate donkeys.

With great effort, Serafina dragged her greying body off the bed. She leaned on the windowsill and peered at the man through a gap in the lace curtains: the smooth shirtless contours of his skin, his blue jeans streaked with the red volcanic earth of Viti Levu. He stamped his feet, shaking the mud from his heavy brown army-issue boots. He strutted the length of the yard, stopping and starting, gesturing and nodding with jerky movements as if giving a violent speech. A defiant speech delivered by a cocky man with a shiny muscular chest. He reminded her of the men in Apolosi's unit: men with ominous intensity, men who either were dead or had fled the country.

Tabua

Apolosi was always destined to be her husband. That's what her grandparents had planned. They had told her about the bloodlines tracing back to the ancestors from Lake Tanganyika on the shores of Tanzania, and the importance of keeping her lineage strong. Bubu had insisted she meet Apolosi in the traditional way. Serafina had protested. She already knew him. They had grown up together, played in large bands of ragged school friends and cousins. They had run along the beaches and sung at funerals. She hadn't seen much of him since he'd joined the army. But she needed no introduction to someone she already knew.

'You have not been introduced with the correct formality,' Bubu would say to her in Fijian, sitting cross-legged on her ornate woven mats, her body curled over lengths of pandanus as she scraped the leaves flat with the edge of a mussel shell.

Serafina obliged her grandparents and accompanied them to the army barracks in Kerpal's taxi. She felt clown-like, clothed in a bright yellow short-sleeved jaba and matching sulu reaching to her ankles and imprinted with neon green airplanes. Bubu had lovingly sewn the outfit for the occasion. Serafina followed Bubu as the old woman walked up the narrow lane to the waiting taxi, bent over at a scoliotic right angle to the ground. Her mind remained nimble, from the constant weaving of intricate patterns held in her vast memory. Serafina believed that weaving kept Bubu alive. She was well into her eighties and the oldest woman in the mataqali. People came to her from many branches of the family to buy her fine woven mats. Every day of her life, weaving. She was dressed in a neat violet sulu and a thin burnt-orange cotton cardigan from New Zealand. Serafina helped her grandmother climb into the back seat of the taxi. Tuwa waited in his black jacket, a bure with a high-pitched roof embroidered on the breast pocket in bright colours, a silken cravat tied nattily at his neck, a fawn sulu va taga fastened over his large stomach and finishing below his knees. He was a tall, old man with a commanding presence, a mata ni vanua, a chief's herald like Apolosi's father. He held the door open for Serafina and Bubu, and then he climbed into the front seat with Kerpal. Serafina felt ridiculous, like a character in one of the overwrought Japanese films she liked to watch before the main feature kung fu movies at the cinema in Suva. Farcical films, surprising and tragic and funny all at the same time. She played along for the sake of her grandparents, and she knew Apolosi would follow protocol and do the same.

At the army base she sat at a picnic table beneath a flight of neatly hewn earth steps, waiting, watching as Apolosi bounced and cantered down each laddered measure. The sun at his back cast him into silhouette. He wore army fatigues: khaki combat pants, black boots and a camouflage shirt rolled up over muscled forearms. A dark green velvet beret obscured his face. Serafina could only make out his broad white smile until he moved closer. Then he transformed into soft eyes, a strong regal nose and high cheekbones. He filled the air above her head. She hadn't looked at him in this way before. Her reaction startled her, and she found to her dismay that she couldn't breathe. Her senses confounded her feelings. She remembered calling him 'dummkopf' when they were at school, a word she had learned from the German nuns.

He sat next to her at the picnic table and thanked Tuwa and Bubu and Serafina for their visit.

Bubu looked at Apolosi across the picnic table. She was dwarfed by the heavy wooden structure and by Tuwa seated at her side. Tuwa sat with both hands cupped over the arc of a carved walking stick. He addressed Apolosi in formal Fijian, and told him of Apolosi's parents' great pride when they had told Tuwa how he had joined the Counter Revolutionary Warfare Unit, and could send money to the village. Tuwa said he knew Apolosi was one of the Commodore's special soldiers, but he said he could not understand why the Commodore 'did' the coup.

Serafina found it amusing that no one could think of an appropriate verb to predicate 'coup'. Staged? Mounted? Perpetrated? He just did it, and we have to suffer the consequences, she thought. She fidgeted and glanced sideways at Apolosi, trying not to laugh at him awkwardly sitting to attention as Tuwa spoke.

Bubu had been watching Serafina, and spoke over the top of Tuwa in her booming bass voice.

'The girl is laughing,' she said.

Tuwa chuckled and slapped his knee.

'Give him the box of food, Serafina.'

Serafina pushed a large banana box across the table towards Apolosi. He opened the box, his muscled arms rippling with unnatural intensity, she thought, as if he gripped it more tightly than necessary for show, for her benefit. The smell of dalo, palusami and barracuda steamed in a hot lovo wafted from the open box. Apolosi spoke to Tuwa in formal Fijian expressing profuse gratitude. Even so, his speech brimmed with nonchalant arrogance, as if he was one who sat at the right-hand side of power. She knew the reality. His was a foot soldier, expendable, like a dog waiting under a table to catch whatever crumbs fell. He stole fleeting glances at Serafina and smiled, his teeth square white blocks against his black skin. The pretence of this whole courtship ritual annoyed Serafina; the pantomime of it all. She remembered her childhood, when she had surpassed him in academic matters. Now he thought he was some kind of big shot in the army. For her part, she felt proud to be on the verge of starting university, and this matchmaking irritated her. Bubu wanted her to get married and have children, and disapproved of Serafina conducting herself like a kaivalagi, wearing trousers to work and drinking cocktails at the yacht club with the Europeans. But she had dreams, and they did not include being an army wife. She wanted to get this charade over with. She wanted out of the bright clothes Bubu had made for the day. She felt sickened to be packaged and presented to Apolosi. But she would perform this duty for her grandparents. On this occasion, family obligation prevailed over her yearning to be modern like women in the movies.

Serafina sat with the required demureness in front of Tuwa and Bubu, listening to Apolosi explain his current military assignment: roadblock duty. Roadblocks had been set up strategically around Suva after the coup, verdant oases of full combat readiness and military show. They gave the city an air of war, unfaithful to its tourist-brochure front to the world. Self-contained battle units with neat tents, army latrines and sandbagged watchtowers. Young men of Apolosi's age manned the checkpoints wearing full battle fatigues and armed with automatic rifles. For a few days after the coup, they would stop vehicles and search for guns, cutting their eyes at the civilians. Traffic moved at walking pace through the roadblocks, forced to navigate around red and white metal tripod crossbars strewn over the road like giant toys on top of the potholes.

Serafina had driven many times through the checkpoint patrolled by Apolosi. The watchtower was built into the base of a hill, and was surrounded by lush greenery and large flame trees. Apolosi guarded the roadblock with three soldiers also known to Serafina from childhood: Josua, Maekeli and Tevita, each wearing khaki camouflage fatigues with an M16 rifle hanging off his shoulders. After many weeks in the unrelenting heat, the soldiers fell into the national malaise like their road worker brothers. They sat around during the day killing time. Serafina noticed this change at the roadblocks: bored soldiers crouching around kava bowls in tight knots of silence; glum, tired ones sitting along the narrow windows of watchtowers staring darkly at the traffic from under their round metal helmets. The populace drove to and from their homes, their work, their kava sessions, their sport, their lives, manoeuvring their cars with slow caution around the crossbars as if trying not to annoy a petulant elder relative. Serafina had listened to Kerpal railing at the delay such stupid monstrosities caused his taxis. But like everyone else, he grew to accept the inconvenience, and began to call out greetings to the young soldiers. Brash tourists began to stop for photographs beside the men and their impressive machine guns. In the end, everyone took pity on the young soldiers sitting in the heat for days. They tried to placate their simmering menace with forced smiles; tried to curry favour by giving them cassava, dalo, fish, kava and cigarettes.

Tuwa and Bubu listened patiently to Apolosi talking about the roadblock. Serafina found it tedious, and sighed with relief when Kerpal returned in his taxi to take them back home. She helped Bubu into the cab, waving goodbye to Apolosi as an afterthought. Bubu laughed as she clambered into the back seat, and told Serafina to go back and say goodbye to Apolosi in the ceremonial way. But Serafina ignored her, and concentrated on a quick getaway.

After their ceremonial meeting at the barracks, Bubu had instructed Serafina to take food to Apolosi at the roadblock whenever she could. She would ride in the silky yellow-cave back seat of Kerpal's taxi and listen to lilting Hindi music played through tinny speakers.

Kerpal could not avoid all of the potholes.

'So many pothole nowadays. Bad for my taxi. They should fix it. Waste time sitting at the road block,' he said.

Apolosi would wait for her at the foot of the watchtower ladder, standing to attention like a guard of honour. He would help her from the taxi with a warm strong hand: an act of gallantry that made her feel like a queen. Then she had to wait in the watchtower, sometimes for hours, while Apolosi and the other soldiers dismantled and reassembled their weapons repeatedly. They could do it blindfold, reciting each step under their breath.

Press rear take-down pin
Rotate upper receiver
Separate
Cock hammer
Press down buffer retention pin
Turn over upper receiver
Pull back charging handle
Lift out bolt assembly
Push out firing pin
Rotate bolt clockwise
Remove
Hold down extractor
Remove pin
Press down hand guard
Lift off

As time went on Serafina noticed that when she came, Josua, Maekeli and Tevita would withdraw and sit drinking kava on one side of the watchtower, talking in whispers and glancing over at her and Apolosi sitting in the corner. She found it unnerving. She asked Apolosi why they acted so secretively and why they whispered when she arrived. He laughed aloud and shook his head. He told her not to be so defensive; to ignore them, their juvenile ways. He turned his back on the three and positioned himself in front of her, shielding her from their gaze. She found herself confronted with the dark smooth curve of his clavicle. She could not look away, and she sensed the ancient Tanganyikans at work.

One day Josua shouted at Apolosi to take Serafina to the barracks and to bring back some oil for the guns.

'We've run out of oil. And while you're there show her how we break down a Yankee gun. Remember to place your hammer in the cocked position,' he said, and he turned to Maekeli and Tevita and laughed.

They laughed along with him.

'And don't forget to rotate your bolt clockwise before you remove it,' he continued, doubling over with laughter.

She marvelled at their lack of decorum. Any semblance of military discipline had evaporated into blue air along with the constant petrol fumes.

'Hey, don't be so rude to me. I know you're plotting something,' said Apolosi.

'Why do you let them talk to you like that?' she said when they were outside the watchtower.

But he hushed her and led her along to the empty army barracks, a weatherboard building made by the Americans in World War II. Its interior was cool. Red hibiscus flowers bordered the perimeter in full bloom. The floors were of polished kauri, and rows of neat bunks lined the walls. The rooms smelled of sun-dried linen. The intoxicating possibility of being caught overwhelmed them.

The man continued to look up at Serafina from Kerpal's backyard. The clattering, dissonant sounds of the day remained loud, punctuated intermittently by a screaming dog. Serafina hated to think about what happened to the dogs. She had seen several of them hit by cars. They ran about the streets scavenging for food, their ribs showing through mangy coats. She felt as though her own ribs showed through her skin. She tried to pitch her body forward to show her face to the man, to see if he would shout something at her. What would he think of her appearing at the window? Would he see her hovering like an illusion? He showed no sign he could see her. She flopped back onto the bed and followed the path of a bright green moko weaving its way across the ceiling, calling out in familiar clicks. She tried to raise herself again to look at the man. She remembered what Bubu had said to her as the curve of her belly had grown.

'Your baby has come from a strong bloodline.'

The young Fijian man in Kerpal's backyard looked like he came from a strong bloodline, a bloodline leading straight back to the Tanganyikan chiefs. An air of resentment tracked the edges of his aura, born of entitlement she guessed. He could be a soldier in Apolosi's unit. Had he come here to search for Apolosi? But that seemed unlikely. Anyway, the men in Apolosi's unit would not find him; he'd fled the country.

When she discovered the pregnancy, they had talked about what to do and had decided to get married. Of course, this had given the soldiers at the roadblock new sport, which Serafina saw whenever she visited Apolosi. They teased him and called him an Indian, and joked about his baby-making abilities.

'Hey Apolosi! How's your Indian son, Kalash Nikov?' It was Josua's favourite jibe, usually followed by Maekeli and Tevita disintegrating into squeals of high-pitched laughter and much juvenile thrashing about.

Josua told Apolosi and Serafina to run away and get married and get out of their way. The three soldiers began to draw into a huddle and stop talking whenever Serafina and Apolosi came near. Apolosi became withdrawn, sullen, and unhappy they'd left him out of their secret discussions. He turned on Serafina; told her not to come to the roadblock any more. She flinched at his unfeeling treatment, and complained about turning into an army wife for him. He reassured her; told her they'd have a good life. After the wedding, she could live on base in the married quarters at QE II Barracks. She knew it would be better for her and the baby to live in the married quarters, where trucks delivered clean water. In built-up Raiwaqa where she lived with Tuwa and Bubu, water stoppages happened frequently, and when the water did flow through the broken clay pipes, it sputtered out of the taps in brown and gritty bursts. Light bulbs and radios flickered on and off because of the intermittent electricity supply. Strange clicks and suspicious echoes during phone calls indicated the presence of regime monitors listening to her conversations with her aunties.

The day of the mutiny coincided with the day of their wedding. In the morning, Serafina had surveyed the stored water. Shelves of old plastic Coke bottles filled with cloudy brown liquid, blooms of sediment gathering in their fat bottoms. She chose the two bottles with the clearest liquid and held them up to the light. Sparkling particles caught the sunlight and danced in suspension before her eyes. She had to boil the water to sterilise it for the marital kava ceremony. She decanted the liquid into a pot suspended over an open fire in the lean-to next to the house. Tuwa lay on his low bed listening to a pocket transistor radio and fanning himself with one of Bubu's elaborately patterned iri. Bubu sat cross-legged over an intricate ibe tabu kaisi, a chiefly mat she had woven for the wedding. She concentrated on combing the bright-coloured woollen fringe at the edge of the mat, pink and blue and yellow and green. Now and then, she spoke to Tuwa in her sombre bass. When Apolosi appeared in the doorway Serafina's heart leapt.

'Did you find a tabua?' she asked.

He handed her a large old whale's tooth with a deep yellow patina. She looked at the grooved lines at the base of the tooth, streaked with dark colour, like dried blood, although she knew it couldn't be blood. The impressive tooth pushed into the palm of her hand, cool and heavy. A looped cord of box-braided sennit threaded through tiny holes drilled at the tip and at the nerve skirt of the old tooth. The intricate woven coconut husk weighed nothing next to the smooth heft of the tabua. Did she sense a cool wind playing along her cheek? She wondered if the spirit of the whale had swum past her face, in languid curves. She knew the spirit of a whale emanated out from a tabua. As if the tooth were still lodged in the whale's jaw and a whale-shaped aura encompassed anyone within the outline of its ghostly body. She sat within the whale's phantom shape and felt its gentle spirit and it calmed her.

'Did you know sperm whales migrate between Antarctica and Levuka?' said Apolosi.

'Thank you Mr National Geographic,' said Serafina.

Apolosi laughed along with her, his eyes velvet brown next to the yellow tabua.

'They are long-range animals. The tooth you are holding has been under the ice in Antarctica.'

Serafina held the tabua to her cheek, felt its smooth cold dentine surface next to her skin and smiled at Apolosi, amused by him.

'If this tabua could speak and tell me about Antarctica, what a story that would be,' she said, smiling at Apolosi, indulging him.

As Serafina unfolded her tapa for the wedding ceremony, she saw Tuwa sit up on the bed, his eyes wide, his fingers turning the volume dial on the transistor radio.

Forces loyal to the military commander Josepha Sanaitalini are trying to put down a mutiny at the Queen Elizabeth Barracks sparked by renegade soldiers who took part in the May putsch led by failed businessman Malo Setonga. The rebel soldiers from the elite Counter Revolutionary Warfare Unit tried to seize the military high command at lunchtime, and are reported to be holding hostages. Nine soldiers are dead and two wounded following a shootout ...

Tuwa shook his head and began to cry. He looked over to Apolosi and said, 'You have to leave'.

Serafina could not believe what she was hearing. Large tears rolled down her cheeks.

Late that night, Apolosi made ready to board an Air New Zealand plane painted with the All Black colours and a silver fern weaving along the empennage. He and Serafina stood and said goodbye through tear-filled eyes, their heads touching. Apolosi held Serafina's hands to his face.

'Look after our son. I'll send for both of you as soon as I can,' he said.

The people-smuggler from New Zealand, Mr Smith, took Apolosi away. A middle-aged, red-faced man with a fat gut and white legs, Mr Smith laughed at any little thing. Always wearing ill-fitting shorts, he had processed Apolosi through his 'system' with glee. Serafina knew Mr Smith. Everyone knew he brought a steady stream of labour from Fiji to work in his orchards in the Bay of Plenty.

'You'll be okay with me Apollo mate,' Mr Smith said, ogling Serafina's growing breasts.

'Thank you,' said Apolosi.

'Yeah, she'll be right. You lot, you drink too much kava for my liking but you'll be right. Lots of money in New Zealand, boy. More than you'll ever make here.'

That same night, the Commodore's soldiers searched out the men in Apolosi's unit, taking to them with batons and machetes. Serafina knew she would not see Apolosi again.

She worried that he had never been out of Fiji in his life. He had never been on a plane. Although he'd had nothing to do with the mutiny, he was a soldier in the CRW, so he'd had no choice but to flee the country. The truth became clear to Serafina. They had kept him out of it, Josua and the others, but they had failed to consider the consequences of their botched attempt at ... what? A counter-coup? Mutiny? Revolution? She didn't know what to call it.

She rang Apolosi the day after he arrived in New Zealand and gave him the bad news. Josua had died in hospital. The Commodore's men had come to her house looking for Apolosi, but Tuwa had turned them away. She didn't tell him the truth about what had happened. She didn't tell him the soldiers had beaten her, and that she had begun haemorrhaging. The sight of so much blood had stopped them. Tuwa had tried to fend them off, but he had failed. One of the soldiers hit him in the face with the butt of a rifle. She didn't tell Apolosi about the baby. She didn't tell him that she had passed out and that the whale had swum into her field of vision and swept past in silence. The baby stayed with her for a time in the whale's outline, lingering in its belly, and then floated away. Serafina listened to the whale singing and followed its plaintive call. She held out her hand and touched the huge triangular tail as it sounded into the depths and led her to safety.

She had taken to her bed. She guarded the tabua under her mattress. Bubu and her cousins gently tended her wounds. She tried to speak to them. But most of the time she lay silent. She had seen Apolosi in her dreams sitting on the whale's tongue holding onto its teeth and steering it under the ice in Antarctica while she lay safe in the whale's belly.

The young man looked up at Serafina from Kerpal's yard. She watched him put on a shirt. Crisp, white, ironed cotton. Why did he wear such a lovely white shirt with his dirty jeans and scuffed boots? She knew after he buttoned his shirt a huge washing machine would swallow him whole and he would magically materialise with clean jeans and shiny new boots. She laughed. Her jeans hung on the wall by her bed, with her dresses and jackets, unworn for many months. She wore a faded and torn nightdress. The ragged material had caught and ripped on her cousin's engagement ring as she had tugged on the turning sheet and moved Serafina's legs.

'Sorry, Fina. So clumsy! Why didn't I take my ring off? Ridiculous!'

Serafina had stared at the girl, blank. She tried to speak, to tell the girl she could not stop herself floating away.

In the evenings, she lay quiet, imprisoned in sound. Endless loops of syncopated jazz. She knew why the music played so loud. The regime needed the music to mask a military raid on her house. The soldiers had orders to find her. While they skulked under the makosoi tree, she would escape through the window. She lay wide awake in a comforting cocoon of mosquito netting ridged with flounced boarders of intricate lace foliage. The branches of the breadfruit tree outside her window would be her escape route. She lay still, terrified. What if rats ate her in the night? Yes, she would escape down the breadfruit tree. She held the tabua to her face as she did every night, feeling the icy cool smoothness of the cementum and dreaming of the whale swimming in a family pod under the ice in Antarctica. She stowed the tabua into a safe pocket cut into the side of the mattress. The whale, a faithful companion, drifted into her peripheral vision and guided her to sleep, sounding into the yawning darkness.

An offbeat jazz piano finished its disturbed rhythm. Serafina wanted to shout at the young man.

"Who are you? When did you arrive? Are you mad?"

A trumpet rose into swinging triplets. She thought the man might talk to her. He lifted his hand in the air and waved, his eyes luminous, his shoulders held back square, and then he turned and walked away, beyond the safe outline of the whale.

Swim Bike Run

With all the challenges it throws at you in so many ways, and in all its myriad forms, I love the race. But I'm dead in the water and so is Karena. We both lived for the race, but it's over for us, and I'm ready to duck if Ravuyalo tries to club me in the head. I'm too fast for him. This race is a river. This race flows without interruption until its inevitable end. You have three options. In no particular order, they are as follows. One, you drop out early from equipment failure. Two, you crash and burn and explode in a huge collision. Or three, and most desirably, you push and struggle through to the finish line and take whatever prize you are given. For most people the prize is the simple satisfaction of getting to the end, even if they come last. Whatever happens along the way, the end always comes. I took the 'crash and burn' option, but I didn't realise it until now.

Karena drove the car from Wellington to Lake Taupō for the start of the race. On a clear day it's a five-hour trip on State Highway One, but it took us six hours in the pouring rain. Harrowing, it was. We always talk non-stop on the way to a race, about the course, the food, my run strategy. This time as we talked we strained our eyes looking through the downpour. I cannot leave out the fact that we did have one big barney, and it played havoc with my mental preparation. The rain fell in relentless, thick blankets: it rained the whole way. As we came through the gorge the rain beat on the roof of the car with a deafening rhythm, and the windscreen wipers swept back and forth in exhausting double time. The uncertainty messed with my mind: not knowing if the race would go ahead. What's the point of training like a bastard if the race is cancelled, right? I kept twiddling the dial on the radio to get updates, but I couldn't find any signal, just alien squealing in between the frequencies. Karena told me not to worry: the race organiser had too much money wrapped up in it, and wouldn't cancel at this late stage. I believed her. Over the years I'd come to rely on her: she calmed my busy mind.

Karena says she loves me. But I know she still holds a candle for her ex, Haley. She dodges looking at me when she tells me Haley sent her an email or a text or rang her. Karena thinks I can't see the bulging in her eyes when she's talking about Haley, as if her excitement is housed in the back of her brain about to burst. She tells me in a by-the-by way in the middle of doing something mundane, parking the car or walking along the footpath. She will say, 'You know Haley, she emailed me today; I don't know why.' I know why and so does Karena, and I tell her why. In the beginning when I first started going out with Karena she'd have 'coffee' with Haley whenever she blew into town, and several times they went drinking together. Can you believe it? My new girlfriend getting drunk with her ex. I felt unhappy about it, and I told her. She didn't do it again, but I get the impression she wants to.

Karena is a drinker. Because of my intensive training, I don't have any inclination to drink with her. Alcohol has its place; don't get me wrong. Beer is a great pre-race carbohydrate load-up, in conjunction with a large plate of pasta. But Karena wants a different type of drinking. She wants the old hoedown, have-a-good-time alcohol session with Haley.

 I kind of understand the Haley thing. There are plenty of times when I wonder about my ex, Bianca. Ah, Bianca. When I first met Karena, I would still meet up with Bianca, to get even with Karena. So we would have these meet-ups, and we'd fall about laughing and forget the horrible names we used to call each other, and pretty soon we would be all over each other right there in the bar or wherever. But then we'd remember that I was with Karena, and Bianca would say in a cutting voice, 'You're an idiot,' and I would be hurt all over again, and I'd remember why we'd separated, and Bianca would tell me to go away. And so I stopped seeing her and concentrated on how horrible she is and how I was so much better off with Karena, who is kind. She holds Haley like a secret little stone in her heart, weighing down every thousandth heartbeat. All that weight will add up one day and sink her if she's not careful. I've heard this from a psychologist lecturer on the internet: she talks about a glass of water, but it's not the glass-half-full scenario. The glass gets heavier the longer you hold it, and she tells you that you need to put the glass down, and the longer you hold it the worse it will be for your arm, because although the glass isn't getting any heavier your arm is going to get sore if you hold onto it too long. The glass represents your worries and your arm is your mental health, or in Karena's case her heart. Heart disease runs in her family. If she has a weak point, it's heart disease. I try to make light of it, to help her dislodge the blockhead from her mind. I mimic Haley's lisp and do the monkey walk to make Karena laugh. Sometimes she gets angry. But I keep trying to make her laugh, and it works most of the time. Now she automatically laughs when I try to make her laugh and it makes her feel good and it makes me feel good.

My ex Bianca encouraged me to have a go at triathlons. She thought it would be good for my health to do something physical, because I have such a high-stress job, working at the emergency call centre. Bianca understood the pressure I faced. Constantly listening to people in crisis is a stressful way to live. They ring emergency services in a terrible state, saying, 'There's a man in my backyard with a gun and I don't know what to do and I'm so scared – please send the police,' and then I have to send the police and stay on the line and keep the terrified person calm and ask them questions until the police arrive. Sometimes I hear people beating up other people in the background or beating up the person on the phone. Sometimes they are crying and yelling that there's a fire or someone is shot or someone isn't breathing, and I have to talk them through the mouth-to-mouth resuscitation procedure or the cardiopulmonary resuscitation procedure. Bianca said I needed a physical outlet to diffuse the stress in my life caused by listening to drama day in and day out. She suggested triathlons. I could run and swim and bike, so I decided to give it a go, for her and for me. I would do anything to please her. My constant need to please and her inability to feel pleased became the problem, in the end.

I went to watch a triathlon race around the harbour, and I loved the excitement of race day. First, I entered a mini-tri, then I kept going from there and entered more and more events, until I graduated to the proper Ironman races in Taupō. Bianca would come and watch me, and we would fall about laughing at the end of a race. We didn't have any serious intentions: we were having a bit of fun, as you do at the beginning of anything new. Nobody aims to be the world champion in the beginning, do they? She didn't race herself. But she loved what the training did to my body: how it made me fit and hard-muscled. After we split up, I kept training. I went to races in towns I had never visited before, such as Wānaka and Whanganui. I didn't place in the front runners – I rate myself as a novice – but I didn't ever come last. After we broke up, I half hoped I would see Bianca in the crowd, watching, so we could fall about laughing at the end like we used to, but she never showed up.

Karena drives me to the races now. She too loves what the training does to my body, my arms. My arms are lean and strong, and I don't carry much body fat. You don't carry much fat if you train hard.

This race in Taupō, it's the biggest race in the calendar for me. I've done it once so far. Leading up to a race I train every single day. Karena has become my coach, although she doesn't have any training to be a coach, and we have had a few disagreements about preparation technique. Despite the intense focus on training, she has become caught up in the competitiveness of the race, and caught up with me. She loves sport, any type of sport, and statistics, and she has a great memory. She remembers my finishing times and she's good on strategy. We talked about rain strategy in the car on the way to Taupō. We talked about whether I should wear the arm-warmers on the bike, how to avoid the crush at the beginning of the swim – we always talk about how to avoid the crush at the beginning of the swim, and how to keep going on the run. The run is the last part of the race and the hardest. My muscles are hurting by the time I get to the run. My energy is gone; I need to refuel with carbs and electrolytes, and Karena is always there at one of the drink stations to hand me a boost.

We arrived the day before the Taupō race started. The rain was incessant. I felt sure the safety considerations alone would force the organiser to cancel the race. But he didn't cancel anything. I breathed a huge sigh of relief when we arrived. I was still thinking about that full-on argument in the car on the way up. The argument started after we drove past a random hotel and Karena said she had stayed there once with dumb idiot Haley, as if I wanted to hear about it. I told her Haley was a dick. Karena tried to defend Haley again, tried to make out they were friends. I told her Haley was not her friend, she was her ex, and how the bloody hell did she think I felt about her going off and getting drunk with her ex. Talk about embarrassing! And how did I know they weren't doing it behind my back. Well, Karena came right back at me and said, how the bloody hell did I think she felt when I went off and drank with Bianca and stayed out for hours and hours and got up to who knows what behind her back? I corrected her right away, pointing out that I'd only had a few drinks with Bianca at the beginning, and nothing happened because I'd learnt from my mistakes, whereas she always met up with stupid idiot Haley whenever she flew into town, and they always took off and got drunk, and for what purpose? How ridiculous! Bianca and I only had a few drinks when we met up, but those two would get falling over drunk, and everyone knows what that leads to: doing it! And if she wanted to do it with Haley when she flew into town, well, she should go off with the dick and we should split up and then she could have her stupid life with moron dickhead fucking idiot Haley fuckwit. They could have done it right there in the bar or wherever, and how the bloody hell did it look for me, the idiot left at home none the wiser? How shameful for me. Karena ended up crying and I ended up steaming and looking out the window. Femmes and their crying! I couldn't get to Taupō soon enough.

There is an art to wet-weather racing. Everything is different, and you want to be careful with the bike. The bike is wet and slippery, the road is wet and slippery, and you have to be extra careful. There have been some terrible pile-ups in wet weather: bikes and bodies everywhere. Running in wet clothing can be challenging; you want to wear as little as possible so it doesn't rub. As for the swim, rain plays havoc with the swim at the beginning.

There is always a mash-up, and visibility is poor in any conditions, rain or shine. Karena's take on it is to swim like a bastard out from the crowd and then veer around again to get a fast line to the first buoy. The swim field lengthens out in the first five minutes anyway, so you need to get into a good group and survive the mash-up without losing too much time. Time is the main issue throughout the race. You want to make good time.

The darkness hadn't lifted when I arrived at the start line on the morning of the race, and even with hundreds of competitors crowded around me, I felt alone. We stood silent in our black wetsuits, waist deep in icy water, waiting for the starter cannon. A ripple of chatter spread through the competitors as we milled about like a herd of restless sea lions. The cannon exploded and I dived into the syrupy black water of Lake Taupō. Underwater I could hear bubbling noises, and my face froze as I pushed my way to the surface and found myself caught in a washing machine of flailing arms and legs. I tried to swim out to the edge of the bunch, barging my way through to get a clear line to the first buoy. But other people swam over the top of me, pushing me under. This is not something you can train for, this pushing and shoving and dunking: you just have to be prepared and fight so you don't swallow too much water, so you don't panic. I pulled on people's wetsuits and slid over bodies, finding a pathway through the morass and swimming into open water. As the pack lengthened out I positioned myself in a group of four in the middle section, a comforting place to be, although I reminded myself not to get too comfortable. I found a good rhythm and kept pace with the other three in my group, popping my head out of the water to get a line of sight to the first buoy. It looked like a big fat inflatable red sausage floating on top of the water. It was at such a distance that it looked small enough to be an actual sausage. The burnt red sausage grew and grew into a looming cylindrical monster as we drew near. A group of swimmers bunched up going into the turn, and I had to push past as we tried to cut close to the giant sausage without getting stuck against the plastic sides. I rounded the sausage and saw hundreds of arms coming out of the water ahead of me, flapping like a flock of black swans skimming the surface of the water in a morning run, off to wherever the black swans go.

The next buoy appeared as an orange dot in the distance which grew bigger and bigger and morphed into a big orange pyramid dancing on top of the water; an out-of-control pyramid that doesn't know it's supposed to be a large solid structure made by the Egyptians to sit there without moving. I joined on to the end of a long ant-line of swimmers in this leg, moving in an easy procession with no interference. The swim turned into a boring exercise in arm rotation and kicking your feet where you need to dig in and do the work and forget about anything else; where there is nothing else to do, nowhere else to be but where you are. The same thing happens with meditation as you try to think of nothing, but thinking of nothing is impossible. Your mind is built to think, and to think of nothing is to think of something. Even a blank screen is still something.

Karena says you have to be mentally fit to get through these times in the race: the times when your mind wanders and you think, what am I doing? I want to go back to bed and go to sleep. And then the orange buoy loomed right in front of me. There were too many people bunched up going into the turn, and we had to tread water in a queue, as you do when you go to the toilet at a concert by a superstar singer who has written music that turned into the soundtrack to your life and everyone else's life.

The water in Lake Taupō is crystal blue glacier melt, feeding from the mountains along thousands of tributaries. The sun came up over our heads, and I could see clear to the bottom of the lake as I swam into shore through fragments of bobbing pumice. I breached the water with a group of other puffing wetsuit-clad people, and we sprinted on wobbly legs up to the bike stands, pulling on the zips at the back of our wetsuits as we ran and trying to wriggle out of their neoprene clutches. I sprinted into the competitors' tent and peeled the wetsuit off my arms, torso, legs. Thousands of us hopped around in the tent, naked and getting dressed or undressed. The volunteers stood back. No one cared about it. We focused on moving onto our bikes. I changed into my bike gear real quick: red Lycra one-piece, shoes with clips to hook into the bike pedals, metallic blue helmet, sunglasses, and black neoprene arm-warmers.

I raced to my bike, lifted it off the rack and headed out onto the bike course. For the first kilometre, I rode through fenced-off sections of downtown Taupō. Crowds of onlookers lined the route and yelled out to us. I looked for Karena but there was no sign of her. Then it started raining again. Riding in the rain is like riding on ice: treacherous. As I slowed my speed around a crowded corner, I saw a tyre come off a bike in front of me. The bike slipped out from under the rider. He fell splat onto the wet asphalt. Several riders found it impossible to avoid him and ploughed into each other, tumbling into a pile-up.

I braked and slid into a zigzag weave, and veered around to stop from piling into them too. My bike almost slipped out from under me but I managed to stay upright, and carried on in a crooked line. From then on, I rode real careful until I reached the safety of the open road. I turned on the speed to make up lost time and found myself at the back of the course where there was no crowd. A few race officials stood on the side of the road holding out plastics cups of water, cups of sugary flat Coke or tubes of carbohydrate gel or bananas.

There are times when you get lonesome out there on the road, but you can't get distracted. You have to pay attention. I started singing a song in my head about being far away and nobody staying around, and why don't people stay in one place, and how good it would be to see you but it doesn't help to know you're just time away. Bianca loved the song; she would sing it to me in a croaky voice. We went to see the singer perform at a concert and she was seventy-one years old, although she'd written the song when she was young. Bianca said it made her remember a time way back in her own life. Listening to it, she'd get weepy, and it would remind her of someone. The tune stuck in my head and kept playing round and round. The best way to get one song out of your head is to sing another song – but then the other song gets stuck in your head, and it can go on and on, but it passes the time. So I sang one of Karena's favourite songs to get Bianca's song out of my head: a song about never opening myself up and living my life my way, and words I don't say, and nothing else matters. We went to see Metallica at a concert in Wellington but Karena said she preferred the version sung by the Vienna Boys' Choir, so we went to see them at a concert in Auckland, on the strength of that one song, and now it's the only song I can remember from either concert. I preferred the wild rocky version at the Wellington concert.

The wind whipped around my head on the way out to Reporoa, the turning point on the bike route, and despite my arm-warmers, my fingers froze and cramped in the rain. The bikes had stretched out into one long single-file line: I was in the mid-field. I had to get over a few mighty hills by standing on the bike pedals and grinding out the distance with my quadriceps. I had trained them well, with Karena's help. She'd come with me to the gym for early morning sessions. We trained in the weight room, with the serious Samoan men who had huge muscles and wanted to be famous Hollywood stars and successful and rich like Dwayne 'The Rock' Johnson. They would lift ultra-heavy weights and spot each other and huff and puff. We would laugh when Karena couldn't lift the same weights as me, and the Samoan men would stare at us and giggle, and we would ignore them. They had strength, but I had the stamina to keep up with them. Karena is much smaller than me. She doesn't have much to come and go on.

Bianca was the same: petite and slight, a stick-insect woman, and if she turned sideways, she disappeared. In fact she was fly paper: if she turned sideways all you could see was the glue, and I was a fly. I couldn't keep away: I was stuck fast and dying. I thought I had better live and get out of that situation. But even now, I feel her pulling me back to her. I've noticed it fading over time, this pull, but I think it will always be there, and sometimes it comes back and hits me when I'm not expecting it. For instance, every year on the first of November, which is Bianca's birthday, I might be driving the car or walking along the road and I remember it's Bianca's birthday. I wonder for a moment if I should send her a text and wish her happy birthday, but I decide not to send anything: what's the point? I've spent time wrestling over it in my head and thinking about her when I didn't want to, but it's her birthday. The same thing happens if I'm doing the dishes: she's there in my head again. She went ape at me one time when I didn't scrub the sink out before I put the water in, and now if I have to wash the dishes she pops into my head. I solved the problem by installing a dishwasher, but the point is she is part of the fabric of my life, and I suppose that's just how it is. The memories popping into your head from other times in your life never leave you: they are part of you forever. I'm not just talking about the memories of my life with Bianca, but every single moment in my whole life: it's all there, a mass of data in a computer. I don't have any control over it popping up. Something will trigger it and there it is, and I'm reliving something. Everything is stored there, and it's annoying, in the same way as it's annoying when you see a lady in a car driving along the road and you can see she has closed the door on her dress and the bottom of it is flapping in the wind as she drives along oblivious. What if the dress gets ripped off the woman by the motion of the wheels, and then she's driving along naked? I understand the pull Haley has on Karena, but I can't change anything: it's part of her. I told Karena that if she wants to drink with Haley then I have permission to keep drinking with Bianca. But what's the point of getting drunk with your ex? So you can lose your inhibitions and try to recapture something you wanted to have but you lost it because you didn't have it in the first place, and if you did have it you wouldn't have split up? Pointless waste of time, I reckon. What you need to do is get on with your training or whatever it is you do in your life, and then over time your grief fades away until it doesn't bother you. I try to explain this to Karena, and she tries to defend herself and I get mad and I tell her to go off and be with Haley then, and be done with it, though Haley already has another girlfriend, and I know it couldn't ever happen. Then it's cold silence and we don't talk for hours.

I picked off points on the bike route to pass the time. I saw a tōtara tree in the distance and counted the seconds until I rode past it. Then I spotted a huge toetoe bush with hundreds of fluffy white fronds. A Portaloo, a flag, another tōtara tree, the top of a hill, the top of another hill, a road sign, a fence post, and so on. This distracted me from the pain in my legs which is a constant feature of the race. The pain doesn't go away, so you learn to accept that it's part of the race, and you carry on and pace it out until the end.

The course is two loops: out to Reporoa and back, twice. You can't cheat: electronic chip sensors are embedded in the anklet they give you at the beginning of the race, and there are sensor mats on the road and they monitor your progress to make sure you have completed the course. There's no subway for you to catch a ride on. I heard a story about a woman who cheated in the New York marathon in the days before electronic chips, although she didn't get away with it. Someone saw her on the train and dobbed her in. I wanted a train to pull up alongside me so I could jump on board; your mind starts to play tricks on you if you live in constant pain. On the second loop through Taupō the crowd had grown. They whooped and hollered and called out the names on our racing bibs. It helps you get through the race without noticing the pain too much.

'Go Alberta!' That's me, Alberta Marāma: Catholic Fijian, lapsed. 'Maraama' with the accented long 'ā' on the second syllable. Not on the first syllable as in the Māori word 'maarama', which means light or moon. Marāma means woman in Fijian. The word for moon in Fijian is 'vula', which also means to be idle or listless or dreamy or lost in fantasies, or carried away by some internal vision, having lost contact with reality. I don't know what the equivalent word would be in Māori for losing contact with reality. Maybe 'pōrangi', although if you are pōrangi you are mad, as in mentally ill.

On the second lap back from Reporoa I pictured myself as one of those little toy cars going round and round on an undulating black liquorice-strap racetrack. I still couldn't see Karena anywhere. I ran into the transition tent and changed into my running gear, and ran back out onto the course for the last part of the race. Three laps of running. At this point, the pain felt unbearable, and all I could think about was getting to the end and finishing. As you start each lap the officials put a different coloured armband on you. White means you have started the first lap, pink for the second and blue for the last lap. I reached the finish line and saw I had a white band and a pink band but no blue band. So I had to go back and run another lap. Your mind gets mushed up. You think you have finished the race and in fact there is one more thing left for you to do. I felt shattered. I had to go deep inside myself to get through it. I counted the seconds and picked off multiple targets. Get past the sound stage with the men in pink Afros, get past the Pride Parade poster of Samoan drag queens on Segways with huge muscles in green and pink and yellow polka dot dresses and matching wigs and silver hoop earrings and sunglasses and gloves, get past the old woman with the poodle, keep moving.

Karena always waits for me at one of the drink stations with a drink and a smile. The thought of seeing her standing on the side of the road cheering me on had kept me going. But I couldn't see her at any of the drink stations on the white lap or the pink lap. I thought she must have been held up somewhere, and that she would be there on the blue lap, the last lap. I looked for her at each station, but I didn't spot her anywhere. As I approached the last station I felt sure she would be standing there waiting for me. But there was no sign of her at all. I couldn't breathe. I began to lose heart: my legs shook uncontrollably and I thought I might fall over. I was worried something bad had happened to her.

Darkness enveloped me when I reached the end. Loud music blared along the chute to the finish line as I jogged through the victory tape: some song about walking hundreds of miles. Race officials with flashlights moved in and gave towels to each finisher, and escorted them to the photographer to get a snapshot before helping them to sit on plastic chairs. They attended to competitors who collapsed on the ground and helped them into the first aid tent.

Karena stood in a corner of the transition tent. I couldn't believe it. She hadn't come into the tent in any other races, and I didn't understand how she could have talked her way past the officials at the entrance. The tent is only for competitors, race volunteers and race officials: not partners or family.

'Karena, what are you doing here?' I said.

'We can go now. There's nothing left for you to do,' she said, and she smiled.

'I looked for you at the drink stations. I couldn't see you.'

'I got held up. I'm so waterlogged. I couldn't get out of the river.'

Her face looked fuzzy. She tilted her head and stared at me for a long time.

'You've done it now. We can go,' she said.

I couldn't move. My legs felt cold and wet.

'Come on,' she said, holding her hand out to me.

I reached for her but she disappeared. I closed my eyes and fell over.

In the car on the way to Taupō, Karena told me she had seen Haley on Facebook the day before and she had seen Bianca in the street on the same day. She had realised that they were part of our lives, but they were in the past, and she wanted to move on with her life with me. She wanted to be happy. She had leaned over, put her hand to my cheek, and smiled. Then we drove into a slip in the road. The car tumbled out of control, and we smashed through a guard rail.

My body jolted against the seat belt and the car plunged over a bank. We crashed into shrubs and flax and toetoe and the windscreen shattered. Shards of glass hit me in the face, and the car hit a tree and rolled over, and we fell into the Tongariro River. The force of the current dragged me out through the smashed window. My blood flowed into the river with Karena's and on into Lake Taupō. My body carried over a waterfall and wedged beneath a rock, and I stayed there for three days, submerged in the icy water flowing from Mangatoetoenui Glacier. Karena stayed trapped upside down in the car until it was time for me to go. Now that I have run the race I can set out on the journey to the jumping-off point and dodge the soul-slayer Ravuyalo, who tries to club us on the head as we run past him to enter Bulu.

I am prepared for the race, now that I really have Karena.

Till

He fell into a blue world. He'd been collecting ice samples with the team, gingerly making his way across the glacier, prodding the snow in front of him with an ice axe to check its solidity before taking a step. The other researchers followed behind him, descending a gentle slope with great caution, their woollen hats bright red against the snow. His axe handle had sunk to halfway, meeting with enough resistance to give him confidence. As he leaned into the snow, his foot sank to the ankle. A deep patch, he thought. But then his foot sank further ... up to the shin, then to his knee, and then he knew he had stepped onto a snow bridge. With a puff of snow, the ice collapsed beneath him, and he dropped into free fall in a rush of blue and white. He landed upright with a hard thud. Snow and ice rained down on his head, leaving him stunned. His left boot was twisted and wedged into a V at the bottom of the crevasse. Pain shot through his foot, ankle, leg. The ankle was broken, he was sure of it. He frantically dug his leg out before the snow's crystalline grip solidified around the boot.

The sheer ice walls around him were dark cobalt, swirling into a cathedral of misty cyan over his head and out into a jag of white sunshine. A few metres along the crevasse, out of reach, the orange weave of his high-tensile ropes rested against the ice, and beyond that he saw the silver blade of his ice axe glinting where it had fallen. He yelled into the azure slit of sky. But he had fallen into an echo chamber, and his voice reverberated and bounced back to him in frightening waves. He slumped against the cold surfaces. That was when he saw her.

Through the shooting pain in his leg he felt surprised at the sight of the woman trapped in the ice wall, her frozen expression one of shock. The skin on her face looked pale as glacial milk. Her skull looked house-shaped: wide towards the top and vertical on the sides, unlike any person he had ever seen. She lay in the hollow of a black rock, suspended in the ice like a forgotten soul in a Stygian canoe. Her ghoulish presence alarmed him. His heart pounded in his chest, although not, he thought for much longer. He wondered how long the glacier had trapped her like human till. Plucked from the upper valley walls and carried into the moving river of ice.

He stifled a whimper of fear and began his safety checks, his analytical brain activating itself like an emergency beacon. Unless his friends found him in this hole and hauled him up, he would die. If he could retrieve his ice axe, and somehow splint his foot, he could haul himself arm over arm, foot-pick over foothold, up the side of the frozen chasm. He moved as far as he could towards the pick, shuffling himself and dragging his injured foot, but the crevasse narrowed and jammed him in and his equipment remained out of reach. He shook himself back to his original position and tried to climb, stamping the crampons of the boot on his good foot into the ice and hauling his hurt foot behind him, but he couldn't find any handholds on the smooth ice. Without his ice axe it was impossible. He was trapped.

The sun inched into a midday glow, turning the sides of the crevasse into lapis lazuli columns and refracting beams of sunshine into the woman's glassed-in rock coffin. The ice magnified her ancient face in front of him. Her body snap-frozen, her mouth open as if caught mid-conversation. Although he was clothed in warm thermal climbing gear, he felt like a mere particle surrounded by frozen pack ice. He yelled out again, trying to gain the attention of the team on the surface. His calls rang against the walls of the crevasse and fell back on him, failing to escape the opening. Surely they had seen him disappear into the hole. But he saw no sign of them. He felt alone with this woman, and the ambient sounds of the ice. He was familiar with the eerie groaning and pinking and the ever-present gurgle and hiss of water echoing throughout the internal plumbing of a glacier. This glacier sounded no different, fizzing and crackling and crunching as it slugged its frozen mass downhill, carrying him along with the ice-encased woman in her black rock canoe.

His head hurt. He drifted into unconsciousness and then back into the crevasse. The woman in the ice looked as if she was moving behind thick sheets of rippling dirty glass.

'You slip or fall? Trip?' she said.

A shrill cry escaped his lips and separated into dissonant notes and descants, which bounced around the cavern walls and settled onto the ice in a light tinkling echo. With a panicked rush he pushed and jerked his body to attention, and tried to chimney climb away from her. Straining his arms against the bulwark of ice, he roared into the void and tried to hoist his body up. He managed to move half a metre before sliding back to the foot of the wall, where he sat exhausted and dejected. Pain seared his ankle, and he breathed in quick steamy puffs. The woman remained frozen inside the wall, poised in mid-air as if calling to her children.

'Do you have children?'

She did not answer him. He noticed a bag tied onto her back, and a copper axe-head fastened to a wooden handle suspended half a metre away from her in the ice. Ancient leaves and a rodent-like animal, with rabbit ears, whirled in iced suspension around her.

He lay back into the soft duck-down lining of his jacket and looked up at the enticing patch of sky above him. Warm salty tears of frustration flowed down his cheeks as he spotted a jetplane drawing a white line across the blue sky aperture. He followed the invisible airplane as it bisected the sky and took people thousands of miles above him on their way home to their families. In the wake of their atmospheric breath he wanted out of this trap.

He watched the distant vapour trail dissolve into cirrus cloud. Turning away he looked to the woman again, and studied her with his academic lens. She was short in stature. There were animal hides tied around her body, and strips of leather fastened in a criss-cross pattern over her feet. Long strands of hair floated about her face, as though she were adrift in the ice. She didn't look like a Sherpa. She was ancient. He was certain she was from an old time: a time of mammoths, and ice sheets. She had been here for thousands of years! Touching a gloved hand to the ice, his thoughts went barrelling back in time to his mother's last day on earth: the day his life had changed.

He had been sitting in the grandstand with his friends. The score: 23 home side, 24 visitors, and home side had the ball. Then he saw his teacher running over. Up the steps. She saw him. And headed … straight for him.

'What are you doing here?'

He should have been in class, not watching the seniors play rugby. But the teacher did not scold him for cutting class yet again. She looked distressed.

'Didn't you get the message? Your mother?'

He ran from the field to the house. Sitting at his mother's bedside holding her hand, his father sat with his head bowed, silent, numb. Her arm felt cold to his touch.

He peered at the woman in the ice. One arm was held across her body as if she was fending off some danger: there was a blade gripped in her hand. He closed his eyes in the cold. After school his mother would always be at the kitchen sink, scouring shiny black seeds out of a ripe papaya or cutting green bele leaves. He'd forgotten that image of her, until now. He'd always tried to hold her in freeze-frame in his mind, her smile or a picture of her on the wall. Now forgotten memories arose from within him, splintering his constructed recollection of her into shards. He saw her delicate hand holding the knife and cutting into the soft amber flesh of a yellow-skinned papaya, its sweet odour heavy in the air. A smile rose into her eyes as she arranged the glistening wedges on a green plate in front of him and sat at the table to watch him eat. He would have been five or six years old. They played the counting game.

'One, two, three, four – and if you eat this one how many are left?'

'Three.'

'And if I cut this one in half, how many are there now?'

'Four.'

He liked her constant counting: counting days, counting time, counting his socks or books, counting the stars. And then there was nothing. Her death didn't fit the mathematical equation. Father plus mother plus grandfather plus brother plus him equals five:

minus mother equals four, right? But after she died he counted zero. Zero stuck fast until time buffeted the worst of the wreckage from his heart.

He was left bobbing in grief's wake, flotsam. He was directionless, floating, washed out. His laziness had brought him here. He would sleep in, and cut school, and his father and grandfather would click their tongues and say, 'If his mother could see him sleeping his future away, she'd have something to say about it.' After her death, he could not forgive himself. When it counted, he wasn't there. He trudged around high school, sat in dark classrooms, and fell asleep with boredom. Then one day in science class, as he sat back with his usual detachment and watched his classmates measuring chemicals, lighting the Bunsen burners, following instructions for a new experiment, he had glimpsed his future. He'd watched entranced as blue copper sulphate crystals emerged at the base of a glass Petri dish. A simple experiment but it startled him: the unexplained materialisation, the perfect gleaming symmetry, the magic. This one simple occurrence moved the world for him again. The garish colours of the periodic table fastened to the wall of the old classroom with yellowing tape came alive for him. He started to see the numeric patterns and trends of valence and atomic radii in the lines of purple and blue and orange and green.

Here there was only blue and white, and her. He heard a rushing sound, the sound of water whooshing into a tube. He'd heard this sound in the spiralling pipe slides at Waterworld. Cold water trickled into the bottom of the V and eddied around his boot. He heard loud gurgling noises, and then a spout of water burst through the wall in front of him and blasted him in the face. Its icy coldness shocked him. He hauled himself up as fast as he could to get away from the rising flood, but it kept filling up below him. He shivered and shook his head and tried to wipe the cold water away with his gloved hand. He could hear blocks of ice around him, crunching against each other as the glacier began to move. He and the woman were moving with it.

'Welcome to the ride,' she said.

'You're not real. You're not real.'

He tried to grab onto reality in his mind. The truth was that his mother had recognised his ability and had nurtured it with the sliced papaya, the endless counting, the numbers. In his last year of school, he'd worked at those numbers, in maths and science. He'd achieved success in these two subjects but failed in others. At the end of high school, he joined the other students in his year clamouring to escape the suffocating coup culture of Fiji. They hawked their prodigious intellects around the universities with no embargoes on Fijian students. Most ended up in Kyung Hee University in Korea and the University of Santiago de Cuba, vying for scholarships to study law and administration and information technology and medicine so they could pursue high-flying jobs in Asia. They knew the junta expected they would return home to work.

'I'm going to Sapporo,' he told his father when he received the news from Japan. 'I want to get out. I want to be free. This is no life.'

'I know,' said his father.

He remembered the apprehension he'd felt as his father and grandfather made arrangements for him to travel to Hokkaido. How he'd gathered with the men of the family around the kava bowl to talk about his journey and how proud his mother would have been. They tried to settle his nerves about travelling so far from home. They gave him dried papaya strips for the journey, wrapped in a cloudy plastic bag that crackled in his pocket. He tried to sleep for most of the forty-eight-hour trip from Nadi to Sapporo. He woke to change planes at Auckland, Seoul and Tokyo. The transit lounges had large windows, from which he'd study the weather and the sky and the clouds of foreign lands. On his arrival in Sapporo the university housed him in a concrete dormitory. He stared out of his bedroom window at a plaza below, paved with uneven flagstones. The heavy fragrance of snowbell trees in bloom at the perimeter of the plaza reminded him of the scent of frangipani flowers in his home town. Flashy green bush warblers zipped in and out of the white flowers, welcoming him with their melodic whistle.

Eating soup from a noodle shop in the plaza became part of the rhythm of his life in Sapporo as he waited for the academic year to start. He found a data entry job in a lab on campus, working for a Japanese postdoctoral fellow in a team led by the foremost expert in Chinese glaciology in the world. His skill with numbers was soon noticed and he was asked to work on statistical analysis. Crunching figures into geospatial metadata, he worked long hours mapping glacial profiles on the Tibetan Plateau. Eventually, number patterns always revealed themselves to him. Gaps and trends emerged from his work. His boss, Hotaka, a young enthusiastic researcher with shaggy black hair and a face tanned ruddy brown from many hours in the sun on Tibetan glaciers, grew more and more pleased with his work. He felt surprised when Hotaka asked him out with the team one night to drink sake.

'I want you to come with us on the next trip to Tibet,' said Hotaka.

He integrated well into the postdoc team. He drank sake with them late into the night as they planned the field trip. He would lose count of how many shots of sake he drank, and he lost count of how many nights he spent in this fashion. He spent the days at his work station entering data into the computer or learning Mandarin and Japanese characters. He laughed at the Mandarin and Japanese characters for 'glacier'. They looked to him like a drunken man careering towards a fence or trying to climb a ladder in comic missteps.

Till

冰川　氷河

Here there was no ladder. No comedy either. Further into the crevasse a fountain of water burst into the air and then gurgled away to nothing. A few icy drops splashed his face. Terror invaded his mind. The ice lurched and chomped around him. The woman had edged closer to him as the ice marched downhill. He unhooked a carabiner from the harness on his waist. With the clip gate open, he chipped at the ice, trying to cut through to the woman's hand and her prehistoric flint knife. But the thick ice defeated him.

He knew that if he was not rescued, no one would find him until his body melted out with the woman at the terminal face of the glacier, where all entrained dropstones eventually emerged and sank into the melt-water sediment. He made the calculation with the surety of his numeric abilities. Taking into account known variables and rates of movement in the glacier, it would take sixty-three years for his body to melt out. Far from his beginnings, along with all the other glacial till and sediment picked up and carried by forces beyond their control. But then, he deserved it. After all, where had he been when his mother lay dying? Her life had ended alone, without fuss or fanfare, lying on a bed. He focused his eyes on the scrap of sky overhead, urging a familiar face to appear, willing that the drifting snow on the glacier would not cover the crevasse over before a rescue party saved him. He could survive another forty-eight hours, not much more.

The crack of sky turned dark in the afternoon, and the woman's face grew dim in the fading light. Popping and cracking noises grew louder, as if the impending darkness had roused the moving ice into a breathing nocturnal monster. He flapped his arms and clapped his hands to his body as the temperature fell. He hoped the stagnant air in the crevasse would provide some insulation from sharp drops in the outside temperature and shield him from the bitter winds above. He huddled into himself, facing away from her, battling sleep. But he couldn't stop his eyes closing, and he drifted off.

A loud crack jolted him awake. He kept still, alert. The gap over him remained open. Distant stars glittered in the shred of sky like a strip of sequins on a woman's black evening dress. With a sudden jolt the ice began to heave. It tilted and tossed him about in a terrifying quake. He cried out in the blackness, flailing and gripping at the icy surfaces but finding no purchase. A block of ice fell on his head and knocked him unconscious.

Warm apricot light encapsulated him as he ate papaya in a steamy tent, the acidic flesh soft in his mouth.

He started awake into a cold reality, with the sun shining into his eyes. His head ached and his vision was blurred. His mouth felt furry and swollen with thirst, and his stomach cramped with hunger. He dug at the snow next to him and brought a handful of cold white to his mouth. The crystals tasted of strange minerals, but he was too thirsty to care. He turned to the woman, and a startled sound came out of his mouth. Her rock canoe jutted out of a broken column of blue next to him. Her upper body had come free of the ice. Her hair hung in bedraggled clumps, obscuring one side of her face. He scrambled and kicked away from her in a seated push as fast as he could dig his one boot into the ice. Breathing in rapid shallow huffs, he heard her speak.

'Wondered when you would wake up.'

He began to laugh hysterically.

'Why, hello ... Tilly,' he said.

'Funny boy, huh?'

Her mouth retained the shape of an open syllable. The milky hue of her skin had dried into deep caramel in patches that had melted free, stretching across her bones like the flesh of smoked barracuda. Sunlight shone through the hole in the snow bridge and onto her face. A drop of water trickled down her cheek, as if she wept. It trailed along her chin and into her fur garment. Long, shaggy fur with a burnt-ochre hue, unlike any animal pelt he'd ever seen except in pictures of one extinct animal, the woolly mammoth.

Her hand poked out of the ice, fingers curled over the wooden haft of the flint knife. The glacier that had for so long enveloped her in a frozen blanket had eased its deadly hold. He hesitated. She was after all an ancestor. Someone's lineage might return to her – many people's lineage, maybe millions – and so he acted with respect for her possible rank in the ancestral tree, parallel with his own grandmother of the nth degree.

Her hand felt as cold as a china plate, inert. He pried the flint knife from her grasp and held it up to the sunlight. Someone long ago had burnished the haft to golden honey. A thin sinew wrapped around and around it to secure a flint blade. The blade was chiselled and flaked to a point in the shape of a leaf, and the edges glowed transparent grey. Now he had it in his hands he didn't know what to do with it. A hunting knife: no good for picking at hard ice. If he tried to stab it into the ice it would shatter into pieces. Instead, he used the sharp bevelled edge of the knife to hack off a sample of fur at the fringe of the woman's outer garment. As he cut the material, a pouch flopped out of her clothing. He caught it in one hand: a wet suede rectangle, with dark ochre stitching. Inside the pouch he could see an assortment of seeds: thousands of round dots in differing shades of brown and black. Some an oversized version of the mustard seed his mother sprinkled into curry, others long and striped like sunflower seeds, and some cylindrical and pointed. His stomach grumbled with hunger, and he wondered if he should eat one.

'Try them. They're good for you,' she said.

'Okay. I will,' he said.

He took the flint knife and used it to cut into one of the flat seeds, exposing the inner kernel, deep vermilion and black. He cupped the stripped germ in the palm of his glove and inspected it. He brought it up to his nose, sniffed it and nibbled at the edge. To his surprise, it tasted like a sunflower seed. He imagined fields of giant sunflowers waving in the sunshine millions of years ago. He separated some of the round seeds into his hand, dipped his tongue in, and chewed slowly. A tingling sensation numbed his mouth with the same heat as pepper or chilli. He rolled the pouch in the mammoth fur with the flint knife and placed it into his jacket pocket. Armed with the seeds he thought he might last a few more hours.

He could no longer see his orange ropes or the ice axe, now buried in the shifting ice. He turned his attention to the copper axe-head still frozen in suspension near the woman. He unclipped another carabiner from his harness and tried to scrape a groove into the ice. He managed to make a slight scratch, but it felt like trying to dig a rock out of a mountain with a needle.

Was that her voice he heard?

He looked up and saw Hotaka's miniature face under a red hat peeking over the edge of the crevasse. He dropped the carabiner and waved and shouted at him.

'I'm here, I'm here!' he yelled.

'I can hear you,' said Hotaka, and then disappeared.

He wanted Hotaka to come back. He yelled up at the sky until his throat hurt. He leaned against the ice wall and ate a handful of snow. He waited and waited, for hours. But Hotaka did not return. He told himself it didn't matter. Now they knew he had fallen into the crevasse, and they would rescue him in no time. He looked at the woman.

Till

'They've found me,' he said to her, and immediately felt stupid.
'Oh?' she said, mouth agape. 'This river will not stop.'

The afternoon passed and the night arrived, and still Hotaka did not return. No cause for alarm. They had encountered a logistical difficulty with the rescue: the altitude, the equipment, lots of difficult calculations to deal with, he reasoned. Clapping his arms onto his body to keep warm, he steeled himself for another night. He ate more seeds and chewed more snow. The next day Hotaka did not reappear.

'I knew they wouldn't come back. They never do,' she said.

'Please ... I've been here for two days.'

On the morning of the third day, he struggled to remain awake. If he fell asleep now he would perish. A snowstorm in the night had covered over the gap above him except for one peephole of sunlight sparkling like a lone star at twilight.

They would never find him now. He had eaten most of the seeds. He looked at her in the dusk light.

'Told you before; this river will not stop. Are you ready?'

And then he heard the rushing sound of water once again. One of the ice walls ruptured, and filled the crevasse with such force that he was swept up into a fountain. Up, up, up into the cavern, bursting through the soft snow bridge. Out of the crevasse one metre into the sky. The geyser dumped him unceremoniously on the snowy slopes next to the hole and subsided. There followed a rapid draining of the water in the crevasse, complete with a toilet flush sound effect. He lay stunned and sodden, looking across the hole at a group of astonished people, including Hotaka and some of his teammates. He gasped for air, winded. He could see his leg, and he fainted at the sight of blood and a fractured bone poking through his ankle.

He woke to a lot of shouting and a hand placing an oxygen mask onto his face while a man strapped the fracture. But he didn't feel any pain, just an aching sadness for the woman. As he lapsed into unconsciousness he vowed he would not leave her behind.

Sixty-three years later, at the age of eighty-one, he took a two-hour flight on a military plane to the Tibetan Plateau dock, followed by a thirty-minute flight in a Zero army helicopter to the glacier. Over the years he had continued monitoring the glacier and its movements. The prow of the rock canoe had begun to surface on top of the glacier near the terminal face, as he'd calculated so long ago. The researchers at Hokkaido University had asked him and his old team to be present as they dug her out of the ice. Only he and Hotaka attended the dig.

She had provided well for them. Among the 174 remaining seeds the ice woman had given him were several ancient species of dinkel wheat that he had cultivated for the seed banks. They produced a strain of high-protein wheat much sought after among health food fanatics. As he approached the site, the crampons fastened to his boots crunched on the ice and reverberated through his feet, and he felt a dull ache at the site of the old ankle injury. He'd thought more and more of his mother as he'd grown older. Now he recalled her laugh, as he beheld the woman rising up out of the glacier.

'Well I'll be ... you came back.'

'I didn't want to leave you here alone in the cold.'

Pigeon Shoot

Somewhere in the plantation a gust of wind sent a hail of coconuts thumping to the ground. A shiver crawled down the back of Litia's neck as she laid a green and white chequered tablecloth on a pandanus mat. Her son Sitiveni drew close to her side. She arranged his favourite food on the tablecloth: golden fried cassava strips, fried eggs and fresh cut weleti, pale pink flesh glistening on the plate. Her eight-year-old daughter Elenoa sat on the woven pandanus mat in an emerald-green sulu and stared at her little brother. Sitiveni pulled funny faces at her.

'Io, masu, let's say grace,' said Litia.

Litia gave thanks for the Christmas holiday they had spent in Fiji, for their safe return home to New Zealand tomorrow, for her brother Wai looking after them in his house, and for Elenoa and Sitiveni's father Bram. Although she and Bram had separated six months ago, she still included him, for the children's sake.

Sitiveni eyed the food and waited for his mother to finish. He fidgeted and blinked fast, holding onto his stomach. He was eager to run into the coconut plantation one last time with his Uncle Wai and his sister. Elenoa folded both arms around her waist and tugged at her clothing. A dim light shone into the rows of spangling on her top, splashing orange reflections into her face and onto the walls around them. Over the past two weeks she had fallen into the rhythm of village life, finding ways to deal with the 'horrible yuckies' as she had called them when they had first arrived: the long-drop toilets, the cold showers and the oily smell of kerosene lamps.

Litia felt glad to be spending Christmas-time in Fiji, although it was hurricane season and the weather swung between torrential rain and temperatures so hot you could fry an egg on the bonnet of a car. The children had shed the layers of clothing they wore in the South Island cold. Shoes, socks and jerseys became relics consigned to the suitcases, and they ran free in the sunshine. Elenoa had stayed outside too long on their first day in the village and the hot sun had burnt her exposed face and shoulders. By the evening, her skin had turned painful red, and her eyes welled with tears. She didn't understand why this had happened to her. She had lighter skin than Sitiveni, but darker skin than her kaivalagi cousins. In Christchurch it was their pale skin that burned in the sun, not hers. To protect her skin from any further damage, Uncle Wai had given her one of his old long-sleeved cotton shirts to wear. She rolled the sleeves up to her wrists and turned up the formal collar to cover her neck. She wore the white shirt everywhere, the scalloped tail flapping out behind her as she walked.

Today Sitiveni wore a yellow bula shirt dotted with tiny blue waves. It hung open, exposing his small brown chest. Litia knew he would throw off the shirt as soon as he ran out of her sight. He shifted on his sit bones, trying to keep his eyes closed as his mother spoke. He found it impossible to stay still. He squinted and then glanced at Elenoa from underneath his long black eyelashes. She poked her tongue out at him. He poked his back at her as Litia said 'Amen'.

'Amen,' they said in unison.

Sitiveni was five years of age, and copied everything Elenoa did. When she picked out pieces of fried cassava and arranged them in a row on her plate like little soldiers, Sitiveni did so too. She sighed and glared at him as she picked up a cassava soldier and bit its head off. He copied her and laughed and made exaggerated chewing movements, his head bobbing to a silent rhythm.

Litia had never before travelled by herself with the children. Bram had always been there to handle the travel documents. She searched in her handbag for the third time in ten minutes and found the black leather wallet holding their air tickets and passports. She glimpsed a dog-eared old snapshot nestling in a forgotten side pocket of the handbag. Wai had taken the photograph of her and the children and Bram standing in front of a pineapple stall in Suva Market. The children were babies. Bram smiled from their shared past, holding Sitiveni with one arm, his other arm draped over Litia's shoulders as she held Elenoa.

Wai looked in through the door, a .22 rifle slung over his shoulder: an old 1960s model with a well-oiled birchwood stock.

'Bula Wai. Have some tea,' said Litia, making space for him.

'No thanks. I think these two want to go to the plantation. Are you children ready to collect coconuts? We might catch a few pigeons to cook in the lovo if we're lucky.'

'Yeah,' they said at once, like identical twins, nodding and smiling at him, excited.

Wai had told them about how delicious the pigeons would taste when steamed in the lovo between a bed of hot rocks and a covering of warm earth and banana leaves, their nutmeg and fruit diet infusing delicate flavours into the meat. But most of all Elenoa and Sitiveni wanted to run through the plantation: a vast, mysterious, wild place they could only enter with an adult.

'We need the hard coconuts for vakalolo, not the green ones for drinking,' said Litia.

'I do know the difference,' said Elenoa.

Litia watched her skip along the ancient moat ahead of Wai and Sitiveni, and then walked over to Aunty Rosa's house across the grass field in the middle of the village. Rosa sat laughing with a group of women surrounded by piles of bele leaves and cassava and dalo wrapped in newspaper and green plastic bags. Litia greeted the women as she gathered her sulu, sat cross-legged next to Rosa, and started peeling cassava for the lovo. Rosa's large, shiny face became larger as she smiled. She wrestled open a plastic bag full of miniature bunches of green globules and tipped them into a bowl.

'Try some nama,' she said, offering the bowl to Litia.

Litia took a tiny bunch of the sea grapes, an aggregate of drupelets like a green boysenberry, and put them into her mouth. They popped as she chewed, and salty liquid burst into her mouth.

'Delicious.'

'Have you decided what to do?' said Rosa.

'I have to go back,' said Litia.

The impasse between her and Bram felt maddening. The children were not happy about constantly moving between their parents' houses on the outskirts of Christchurch. They found the transitions difficult to manage. One time Elenoa forgot her homework at Bram's and he had to drop it off. Another time Sitiveni forgot his raincoat at her house and she had to take it to school for him. Elenoa questioned her and Bram about the need for the divided living arrangements. Litia knew Bram weaselled out of explaining it to her, and would say to Elenoa, 'Ask your mother.' Faced with her daughter's questions, Litia told her, 'One day the situation might change.' Elenoa asked when the situation might change, and how she might change it. At this, Litia resignedly told Elenoa to go outside and leave her to sew. She had no words to describe to Elenoa the untenable nature of her relationship with Bram.

She felt that, ever since Bram's father died, he had lost heart. He never talked about it, he never helped with the children, and he spent his time married to his DOC ranger job. When she pressed him he agreed that he found life difficult; that they were like ships passing in the night. But he wouldn't do anything to help solve the deadlock. The atmosphere between them had grown oppressive and silent, and it had started to affect the children. In the end, Litia couldn't live with his cold indifference any longer, and she had taken the children and moved out.

'Why don't you stay here? There's the convent school,' said Rosa.

A salty breeze wafted into the room through the hinge-board windows propped open with pieces of wood. Litia felt the air move past her face. She watched as the draught caught the newspaper wrappings, ruffled up against the plastic bags and then stilled. She suspected the reality of walking along the beach and swimming across a river to get to school would soon wear thin for Elenoa. The children at the convent school had no tablets or computers, unlike the children at Elenoa's school in Christchurch.

'Bram won't allow it. He's so stubborn. He wants them back in New Zealand.'

'What if you live here and send the children to Christchurch to live with him?'

Litia didn't want to admit she had contemplated this option. Giving up her children. What kind of a mother does that?

'I can't live here without them. Anyway, Bram said he won't quit his job to care for them.'

The women murmured and shook their heads.

'He loves being out in the fresh air. Doesn't want to be stuck at a desk in Christchurch.'

'He's a park ranger, eh?' said Rosa.

'Io, dina? What does he do in the park?' said Aunty Mere, her dark eyes sad, her hands stopped in mid-air.

'Lots of maintenance work. He fixes bridges and tracks, and in the summer he takes tourists hiking on the glaciers along the West Coast.'

The women looked puzzled, and questioned Litia. Tourists they knew about, working as they did in the sprawling hotel built on village land, for which the village council received a hefty annual rental from the Japanese leaseholders. But glaciers? What is a glacier?

'They're huge rivers of ice, as long as Pacific Harbour and as tall as the new mall building in Suva,' said Litia.

'Wow, so grand? Must be cold, eh?' said Mere.

'What if you split the children? You live here with Elenoa, and Sitiveni could live with Bram in New Zealand? They could swap over in the holidays,' said Rosa.

Litia tossed a furry brown dalo with a deft turn of her hand, rotating it and slicing off the skin.

'The air fares would be too expensive: a lot of travel back and forth. I'd miss Sitiveni too much. And Bram wouldn't agree to it.'

A distant gunshot echoed in the plantation. The women stopped peeling vegetables and turned their heads in the direction of the popping sound.

'That was quick. They found a pigeon already?' said Litia.

'Vakalolo pigeon. Sa vinaka,' said Rosa.

The vegetable peelings grew into a mound on the floor as the women worked steadily and talked and laughed. Rosa instructed two young girls to gather the peelings and take them out to the compost. The girls wrapped the dirty heap into a newspaper bundle and carried it between them to the doorway. But they hesitated on the threshold, their attention drawn outside. The newspaper package dropped out of their hands, spilling its contents onto the steps.

'What's wrong?' said Rosa.

The smallest of the girls pointed out the door, her mouth a dropped O, her eyes enlarged. Litia was wrapping dalo in tinfoil. She heard shouting and screaming from the field. Rosa stood up and walked over to the door to look. She gave a stifled shout, and then she ran. Litia and the other woman crowded to the door.

'What is it?' said Litia.

She saw her aunt running. Then she saw Wai holding a bright yellow and blue and red bundle. People streamed out of their houses and ran towards Wai. She started walking towards the commotion and broke into a sprint as her eyes confirmed the bundle was Sitiveni, limp and bleeding in Wai's arms. She saw Elenoa running along the moat towards her.

'Someone call an ambulance!' said Wai.

Rosa ran towards the priest's house, where there was a phone. Wai carried Sitiveni through the middle of the village and into his wooden house. As Litia reached the house, Wai lay Sitiveni onto one of Aunty Rosa's fine woven mats. Wai hugged himself and made a wailing noise. Litia screamed and fell to the floor next to her son, crying.

'No, no, no.'

Sitiveni's chest was red with blood.

'What? How?'

She put her hand on Sitiveni's small chest, trying to staunch the blood flowing out of his body.

'I left the gun to get a stick for the coconuts. I left it and they picked it up and it went off.'

Wai blubbered and rocked on his heels. Litia looked up as Elenoa appeared at the door.

'Elenoa, what happened?'

Elenoa looked around the room at the blood trail on the floor and the blood on her shirt. She couldn't speak, and ran away.

Litia sat in the back of a speeding ambulance watching two Kanaky medics work on Sitiveni. Wai and Rosa followed in the red dust wake in a beaten-up old ute. Litia watched helplessly as the medics spoke to each other in frantic Kanaky. They tried to revive Sitiveni with CPR and mouth-to-mouth resuscitation. They shocked his little body with a defibrillator. But his heart would not restart.

'I'm sorry. He's lost too much blood,' said one of the medics.

Litia sat motionless next to the gurney and held Sitiveni's cold hand. His brown eyes looked up at her, still as well water.

Litia tried to call Bram from the hospital. The DOC manager tracked Bram on GPS to a hiking trail on Fox Glacier, but couldn't raise him on the emergency radio. But he assured Litia he would keep trying to get a message to Bram. She returned to the village in the ute with Wai and Rosa. They huddled together, silent, their bodies knocking against each other inside the cabin of the ute as it bumped over rutted dirt roads, while Sitiveni lay cold in the morgue. The Divisional Commander of the Fiji Police entered the village with a retinue of police officers in three large trucks. He looked young and light-skinned. He wore a navy blue felt beret with the red crest of the Fiji Police stitched at the apex. He turned over the .22 in his hands.

'Is the gun registered?'

'No,' said Wai.

'Take me to the crime scene!' said the Commander.

'"Crime scene?" What do you mean?' said Litia.

The Commander cut his eyes at her but did not answer. Wai gestured towards the plantation.

'This way.'

Litia watched Wai walk along the moat pathway, this time trailing the Commander, with several police officers in tow. A few village children tried to follow the procession, but a police officer waved them away. Litia took Elenoa's hand and led her into the house with Rosa and several police officers. She settled Elenoa on the mat next to her while Rosa lit the stove and offered tea to the men, their uniforms darkening the room. They declined and sat inscrutable and cross-legged.

The Commander marched up the front steps of Wai's house with a stern look on his face. He held the .22 at his side. His subordinates stood as he entered the room.

'We are taking you and the girl and your brother to the station for further questioning,' he said.

'Why do we need to go to the station? My son is dead,' said Litia.

The Commander ignored her and strode out, nodding at his men. Rosa helped Litia collect her handbag and a jacket for Elenoa, and Wai waited for them in his bloodstained shirt. The officers escorted them from the house to the waiting trucks. Everyone in the village gathered and watched from a safe distance as the police officers helped them into the uncovered tray of the largest vehicle. Three officers crouched with their backs to the cabin holding long rifles upright against their shoulders. Litia and Elenoa sat on the hard steel floor and held onto the sides as best they could during the bumpy ride. Wai positioned himself on the wheel housing, his hands gripping onto the side of the truck as he stared into the middle distance. One of Rosa's nephews drove her in the ute, and several other trucks from the village followed the police trucks at a safe distance.

At the police station, a scruffy building next to the hospital, a police officer separated Litia and Elenoa from Wai and led them into a concrete cell painted dark green. The room smelled of damp and mould. A rusty chair lay on its side on the floor, and a flimsy metal table leaned against one wall. Litia thought someone would come to interview them. But as the hours passed she began to wonder if the police had placed them in custody. They sat on the hard concrete floor and Elenoa went to sleep with her head in Litia's lap. At 11 o'clock that night, when Sitiveni had been dead for half a day, Litia heard a grating sound as a key turned in the lock. The door creaked open and the Commander walked in. He planted his feet astride with his hands behind his back and glared at Litia sitting fearful on the hard floor. Elenoa huddled into her mother, groggy and tired.

'We have charged your brother Waisake with manslaughter and contravening arms and ammunitions regulations. We are holding him in custody,' he said.

'But why? He did nothing.'

'We are also looking at charging you and your daughter with negligence.'

Litia stood up with Elenoa and they hugged each other. The Commander shifted his attention to Elenoa.

'Why did you run away?'

'I didn't,' said Elenoa.

'What did you have to hide, eh?'

Elenoa said nothing, her eyes terrified.

'Innocent people don't run away.'

'She didn't hide,' said Litia.

The Commander's eyes narrowed.

'You people come over here from over there and you think you're above the law. I am the law here. This is not New Zealand.'

Litia fell silent.

'You may go now. But we'll be in touch.'

Litia ushered Elenoa out of the musty room. She was relieved to see Rosa waiting outside the police station in her black sulu and jaba, sitting on the kerb next to the ute with her nephew sprawled out asleep in the shadows.

Upon their return to the village, Litia saw the village council had gathered in the large bure. The elders sat impassive around a large bowl of yaqona in the middle of the room. A young boy sat cross-legged in front of the yaqona bowl handing a coconut bilo of the brown liquid to another boy to pass to the elders. The young men sat around the edges of the meeting house listening to the speeches. Litia heard her cousin, Ioane, the village chief, speaking. She listened from outside the open walls of the bure.

'It was a tragic accident. The police are wrong to charge Wai,' said Ioane.

The village elders mumbled among themselves. Litia knew the risk he took criticising the police around the yaqona bowl.

'We are powerless to do anything,' said one of the elders.

Everyone nodded and murmured in agreement. One of the younger men spoke up.

'The Commander can arrest any one of us if he wants to. We all have relations wasting in Naboro Prison because they dared to speak against the Commander.'

Litia expected the men would talk late into the night. She walked on to Wai's house, where the women had gathered wearing black sulu and jaba. They stayed the whole night, drinking cups of tea, eating cake and sleeping on mats. Elenoa sat with her mother, her eyes blank. She didn't stir until Rosa massaged her hands and gave her a bitter green drink to help her sleep. Litia carried her to a bed in the corner of the room and pulled the mosquito netting closed. She lay on the edge of the bed and fell asleep next to her daughter, exhausted.

Bram arrived at the village the following day. He had come straight from the glacier. The ice glare had burnt his face golden brown, except for snow-goggle circles around his eyes. His brown hair was spiky and unkempt, his face drawn and heavy. He carried a blue daypack and wore a green DOC shirt and tramping shorts and boots. Litia was shocked to see him. She fussed with her clothing, and felt unprepared. She had not expected him to arrive so soon, and worried the house was not ready for him. Elenoa hid behind her mother as Bram approached.

'Litia! What happened?'

She couldn't answer him.

'Elenoa, come here,' he said gently.

Elenoa shook her head and buried her face into her mother's side.

'Say hello to your father,' said Litia, reaching her arm around to her daughter.

Elenoa peered at her father from behind her mother's waist and said, 'Hello.'

Bram looked at his daughter, and she ran into the house. Litia took his hand and they fell into each other, sobbing.

'Where is Sitiveni?' said Bram.

'He's ... he's ... in the morgue.'

They had not held each other for such a long time. She'd forgotten the broadness of his shoulders, the smell of pine trees ingrained into his DOC uniform, the safety of him. She regained her composure and looked about. The villagers were looking and whispering. She pulled back from him. With the clarity of cold mountain air she realised that she always pulled back from him, always before he did. She felt ashamed of it now, and went to touch his cheek, but he had already turned away. The women fussed over him, the kaivalagi from New Zealand.

'Make him a cup of tea,' said one.

'Move, you kids. Let Ratu Bram sit,' said another.

He tried to cross his stiff legs. Rosa brought out the only chair in the house.

'No, I can sit on the floor,' he said.

He leant against a wall and stretched his legs out in front of him. Litia laid the tablecloth and Rosa placed a cup of tea and a plate of scones before him. He told them he didn't feel hungry, but he sipped the tea and ate a scone. The women left the room, leaving Litia and Rosa and Elenoa and Bram alone. Elenoa stayed close to her mother and watched her father. Bram smiled at her. Several children lounged on the steps outside and leaned into the room over the lip of the doorway. Aunt Rosa shooed them away.

'Lako! Lako!'

The children gracefully unfurled themselves and walked into the sunshine.

'We can have him back tomorrow. We can bury him here next to his grandfather,' said Litia.

'Why? He was born in Christchurch, same as me, and my father ...' said Bram.

Litia began to cry, and Bram moved across the mat and put his arms around her. Over Bram's shoulder she watched her daughter stiffen at the sight of her parents embrace, and saw a reflection of herself. She was the one who had run away. He had not abandoned her, she thought. She had abandoned him! She was the one who had complained that she felt marooned in the cold and white of his hometown. She had frozen the conversation.

She had locked the deepest part of herself in a glacier, like those he loved so much. She reached for his hand and locked her cold fingers into his warm gentle ones. Looking into his sad eyes, she melted into him and stroked his hand, kissed his cheek. She no longer cared if the villagers saw.

Rosa sobbed into a silk scarf Bram had given her. Elenoa teared up as she watched her parents. Deep in the plantation a coconut fell.

'I killed him,' she said.

Litia and Bram broke apart.

'No you didn't, Elenoa. It was an accident,' Bram said.

'How would you know? You weren't here. You're never here,' she said.

Her shoulders shook and convulsed as she wept.

Litia pulled her daughter close and said, 'Elenoa, he's with Bubu and your grandfather now. They'll look after him.'

'This is worse than when Bubu died, much worse. Bubu showed me how to climb trees, and she ...' her voice trailed away and she slumped against her mother, crying.

'Come on, let's get you into bed.'

Litia led Elenoa to her bed in the corner of the room and tucked her under the sheet. She watched Bram from behind the mosquito netting and listened to the noises of the coconut plantation in the distance. Long tree trunks creaked and knocked against each other, pigeons barked in strange tones, and the ominous thuds of coconuts echoed as they dropped to the ground, one by one.

The next day, in Wai's house, Ioane sat on elaborately woven Lauan mats with his two brothers, trusted advisors. Rosa's nephew sat in the middle of the room dipping a smooth coconut bilo into a clay dari. He filled the bilo and poured the muddy liquid back into the dari several times to mix the yaqona. He passed a full bilo of yaqona to Bram, who cupped his hands together and took the shell, draining it in one draught, his face contorting with the bitter taste. Ioane swivelled a box of matches in front of him on the mat.

'I've spoken to Father Michael. We can hold the funeral on Saturday,' he said.

'What about Wai?' said Litia.

'Can we get him out on bail or something?' said Bram.

'They charged him with manslaughter,' said Litia.

'That's stupid,' said Bram.

'I don't know what to do,' said Litia.

'We are going to see the Commander tomorrow. He's related to my wife on her Lauan side,' said Ioane's younger brother.

'Would money help?' asked Bram.

'Oh yes. In this situation, money would definitely help,' said Ioane.

'I have some money with me.'

'Good. Then I think we can convince the Commander to let him go. After such a tragic accident I'm sure the Commander can see … reason,' said Ioane.

Litia hoped it would be true: that Wai would be freed. This was how it worked, she knew.

But her son was dead, and she didn't know how she was going to get through it. She was glad to have Bram with her, and Elenoa.

Bram looked different. He stood up, his face ashen, and lurched into the yard. Litia ran out after him. He dropped onto his hands and knees. She rubbed his back as he vomited into the grass. He got up and stumbled over to a frangipani tree.

'I want to see my son,' he said.

He fell on the ground face down and sobbed, inconsolable among the dead and bruised frangipani flowers. Litia lay on the grass next to him and gazed at the sky.

'We can visit him today,' she said.

Bram lay still. She could hear the sea crashing onto the outer reef. She placed a hand on his shoulder. They stayed in the garden, and when the sun had moved through the leaves of the frangipani tree and into the afternoon, Bram sat up and looked at Litia as she lay on the grass.

'What were you doing on the glacier?' she said.

'I hiked in to help a rescue team. They found a man. Part of a group climbing an icefall. He fell and died. We had to carry him out. His family were waiting when we brought him out. He had a son, a young son, sitting there in the car park crying for his father, and I started crying and ... and ...'

He took her hand and lay back onto the grass beside her. They listened to the sound of coconut fronds swaying in the breeze. A sun shower sprayed them with a fine misty rain as they looked into the sky.

'I've been thinking about us,' he said.

'Me too, Bram. Me too.'

Rabbit Shoot

To help her break the news, Sally recruited Imogen's favourite: Vegemite toast soldiers laid out in a perfect row. She could see Imogen knew something was up, from the way she glanced at Sally and held herself more rigidly than usual as she entered the kitchen and smirked and placed herself on a high stool at the breakfast bar in front of the plate. Rows of orange spangling on Imogen's leotard flared in the morning light slanting in through the window and reflected into her eyes like flames. She looked sideways at the strips of toast arranged in exact military formation, side by side, all the same length and width.

'What's this?' said Imogen.

Sally regarded her daughter with dismay. At eleven years old, her well-honed suspicion about the motives of adults was on high alert in the face of Sally's aberrant joy.

'Oh, I just thought you should have something substantial before the competition.'

Imogen picked out a strip of toast and dipped its head into the yolk of a decapitated egg. At least she was eating, thought Sally, sighing with relief as she busied herself at the bench straightening the herb jars. When sage lined up with tarragon, she leaned on the bar and met her daughter's leery glance. The puff went out of her resolve as it converged with the weight of what she wanted to say to Imogen. She pulled at a loose thread on her sleeve.

Until now, Sally's life had been a series of calculated risks, each one an attempt to rebel and break free from the compulsive strictures her mind had always imposed on her. But each time she failed to free herself. Each time she only succeeded in giving acceptable form to the chaos so it could operate freely within known boundaries, destroying her from within like a hungry rat making landfall on a predator-free island. At seventeen she had taken a calculated risk with one of the cool boys at school. He had an open face and a huge smile and a goofy, loping gait. He drove an old holden with gleaming hub caps and she sat close to him in the front seat. He was her first attempt at rebellion, and that particular attempt resulted in pregnancy. She found herself trapped, alone within the world of solo motherhood: a place where people expected a woman to impose benign order upon chaos. Wake up, feed the baby, wash the clothes, fold the clothes, change the nappy.

Imogen's father didn't help Sally at all. He lived for the road, and had dropped out of school and found work driving long-haul trucks for a cattle-feed company. Now and then he'd blow through town and take Imogen to the park or walking along the look-out path, or over to the playground to play in the castle. He was such a kid. The last time he'd visited he'd told Sally he wanted them to be a family. She felt secretly thrilled, but didn't want to look too eager and jeopardise the possibility.

'I'll think about it,' she'd said, as Imogen ran into the room clutching a Barbie doll.

'Think about what?'

'Your father might come and stay with us for a while.'

'Oh?'

Imogen threw the doll on the ground and stamped on the pink plastic head.

'I want to go to the castle playground,' she said, pouting.

The accident had happened on a busy road near the playground. Imogen's father was killed by a speeding car. Emergency services found Imogen sitting on the curb, unharmed, playing with her Barbie dolls, arranging them in headless rows. Their heads were behind her, lying in a circle on the grass, all face down.

The untimely exit of Imogen's father thwarted Sally's plan to escape, to bring his brand of anarchy to bear on her compulsive order.

Aunty Nora became unwittingly complicit in Sally's next tilt at escape. She encouraged her, supported her with money and babysat Imogen while Sally attended classes and went on to qualify as an accountant. Sally knew that if there was ever a profession in which it was acceptable to aggressively impose order upon chaos, accountancy was it. She wrangled numbers, stacked reports into neat piles and kept her desk freakishly clear. Her work colleagues considered her hard-working and virtuous. They admired her obsessive need for order, and excused her quirky habit of walking up and down the steps three times before entering the building. But they didn't know how she battled with herself. She spiralled down into the numbers, tighter and tighter, finding no relief.

Allan was her great new hope for salvation. When they'd first met she'd told him she was a stickler for detail.

'I understand. You're driven,' he'd said.
But that wasn't quite what she meant.

Sally pulled at the loose thread on her sleeve until it snapped.
'So ... I have some good news,' she said to Imogen.
Imogen gulped and tilted her head to one side.
'What news?'
Sally heard Imogen's mocking tone, but she carried on.
'You know how long we've known Allan. Last night at dinner ... Last night, well ... Allan asked me to marry him, and, and ... I said yes. We're going to have a wedding.'
Imogen's eyes narrowed.
'Whatever!'
She glared at her mother as she picked up the last hapless soldier and bit off its head.
'Will you do it in your bed?'
'Imogen.'
'Where's my turquoise leotard?'
The sun had moved, and the light hit Sally in the face. She brought her hand up to shield her eyes.
'Does Ed have to be my brother?'
'Ed will be your stepbrother.'
'He better not get into my room.'
Imogen rushed out, leaving her plate on the counter littered with breadcrumbs and congealed egg.

The icy atmosphere lingered for the entire car ride to the Gymnastics Club. The reveal – or more accurately Imogen's reaction to it – had frayed Sally's nerves. She found herself driving with excessive caution, as if an animal might jump out in front of the car at any moment.

Rabbit Shoot

'Do we have to live with them?' said Imogen as they turned into the car park.

Sally inhaled with the fright of Imogen's question and narrowly missed the bumper of another car as she veered into a parking space. She turned off the ignition and tried to sound calm.

'We'll live together at the farm, all right?'

Imogen sulked, hunched her shoulders and glared at her mother.

'If Ed ever touches any of my stuff ...'

She slammed the car door as she exited. Sally followed meekly, carrying Imogen's gym bag to the team seats at the end of the hall. She flinched at the familiar squeak of floorboards as young gymnasts with chalked hands and taped feet ran, vaulted and limbered up for the competition. Allan entered the room, tall and solid, holding Ed's hand. They had identical haircuts, close-shaven at the back and sides. Sally waved to Allan, self-conscious, aware of Imogen's surly look.

'After prize-giving I'm going to Aunty Nora's for a dress fitting,' said Sally.

'What about me?' said Imogen.

'You can come with me if you want.'

Imogen pouted and folded her arms as Allan arrived and kissed Sally on the cheek.

'Or you can go with Allan and Ed and spend the afternoon at the farm,' said Sally.

'Yay,' said Ed, jumping and clapping.

Allan smiled, showing his large teeth.

'Great. We'll go into the back field and catch a few rabbits for dinner if we're lucky,' he said.

'Oh? The whole day, right?' said Imogen, her eyes on Sally.

'I'll pick you up when I've finished at Aunty Nora's, okay?'

Imogen scowled and said nothing. She turned and ran over to her giggling teammates, resolutely ignoring Sally for the rest of the morning.

Sally and Allan clapped and shouted encouragement as Imogen finished each event. Her stepbrother to be, five-year-old Ed, attended the toddler's class at the same club: he'd learned to perform a forward roll. He jumped and cheered and watched Imogen with adoration. She ran at the vault with frightening speed and launched herself into a handspring which somersaulted her into the air in a perfect arc. Without any help from the coach, she performed a near flawless dismount from the uneven bars, and completed the competition as the club champion, a star. Sally smiled at Allan as the prize-giving announcements echoed through the hall.

'How did she take it?' he said.

'She finds it difficult, since her father died, you know.'

Allan nodded and waited, but Sally had nothing more to say. She stayed to watch Imogen collect the club trophy, and then hugged her goodbye and left for the dress fitting. The drive over to Aunty Nora's home on the other side of town took Sally almost an hour, when it should have taken twenty minutes. She kept checking in the rear vision mirror, fearful that she'd hit someone and that their body would be lying in the road. As she approached Nora's road she thought she had hit a dog, and needed to pull over and get out and check. Of course, there was no dog; there never was. She edged herself back into the car and tried to refocus her attention onto thoughts of her dress: the fall of the material, the placement of the rhinestones, anything other than driving. Driving always drew it out of her when she was stressed.

Nora had converted the garage at the back of her house into a workshop. She sat on a wide bench seat in front of a sewing machine in the middle of the floor, surrounded by bolts of material. A rack of wedding dresses in differing shades of white and cream stood in the corner. There was a lone black dress at the front of the rack.

'A black wedding dress!' said Sally.

'I have some Goth clientele. I made my first one years ago for the niece of a woman at church,' said Nora.

'Gothic! Not for me.'

'No, yours is classic cream satin.'

Nora swept the black dress aside and withdrew a coat hanger holding a half-made creation, a simple A-line halter design with a puddle train and rhinestone beading around the neck and waist. Sally had ordered it several weeks ago.

'Do you like it? I need to adjust the seams,' said Nora, moving her ample girth around Sally.

'Oh, it's more beautiful than I imagined.'

As the dress fell over Sally's head she felt a pin scratch deep into her finger.

'Ouch!'

'Sorry,' said Nora.

Blood drops fell onto the inside of the waistline. Sally pressed a tissue against her punctured white skin.

'The bleeding won't stop,' she said.

'Here, this should fix it,' said Nora, wrapping a cut-off piece of cream satin around Sally's wounded finger.

'How's Imogen?'

'She's fine. You know how she is,' said Sally, suddenly tearful.

'I'm sorry,' said Nora.

'I don't know what's come over me.'

'Imogen will be fine, Sally. She's doing well with the gymnastics, isn't she?'

'Oh yes ... she's on track for the New Zealand team this year.'

Sally's phone rang in her bag. She stood dejected, her unfinished wedding dress hanging from her hips, the patch of blood showing on the waistband. Nora handed Sally the ringing bag. She couldn't find the phone. The ringing grew louder and more insistent. She found it and thought she saw Imogen's number on the small screen, but the phone stopped ringing as she answered it.

'Imogen? Ah ... too late!'

'So annoying,' said Nora.

Sally was about to ring Imogen back when the phone rang in her hand. She dropped the device as if it had given her an electric shock. She watched helpless as the phone slid down the satin material and hid in the cream puddle at her feet. Nora bent with great effort to retrieve the phone, and handed it to Sally.

'Hello Imogen?'

'Sally, it's Allan.'

'Allan? Are you all right?'

'Ed's been shot.'

'What?'

'Ed ... he's ...'

Sally screamed. 'Imogen!'

'Imogen's fine.'

Nora drove Sally to the farmhouse. As the car entered the farm gates Sally could see an ambulance backed up to the front of the house, its doors flung wide open, bright lamplights shining onto the house in cold hospital brightness. Police cars were parked askew on the front lawn. Sally heard the police radios beeping and hissing as she and Nora walked towards the house. Two medics carried a gurney out of the front door: a pair of tiny feet peeked out from under a bloody sheet. As Sally walked past the front of the ambulance she heard the driver talking on a radio.

'Yep, taking him to the morgue now. It's a Kennedy shot. Point-blank through the forehead: exited the parietal.'

Sally broke into a run up the steps into the house, down the hall and into the lounge. Allan sat red-faced on the couch. Two men in suits stood over him gripping notepads in their hands, and a police officer in uniform stood at the door as she entered. Allan looked up at her with tear-filled eyes, and she ran to his side and hugged him. The police officers looked at their feet, embarrassed.

'Where's Imogen?' she asked.

'In the kitchen,' said Allan.

'You must be Sally Randerson?' said one of the suits.

'Yes.'

'I'm Detective Inspector Crane from CIB.'

The detective, a large, middle-aged man with short-cropped hair, wore a dark suit, a navy blue tie, and a wide-collared pale blue shirt. His face, long and clean-shaven, looked like the police officers Sally had seen giving television interviews. Imogen appeared at the doorway with a police officer who led her to the couch. Nora followed, holding a tray laden with cups and a steaming pot of tea. She placed the tray on the coffee table and began pouring tea into cups and handing it out to the people in the room.

Detective Crane emphasised that the police viewed the incident as an accident, a tragic accident, and that no charges would be laid. But he said that he would need to report Ed's death to the coroner. At 11 o'clock that starless night, when Ed had been dead for half a day, Sally decided to take Imogen back to her house to have some rest. They had been at the farm with the police since the afternoon.

'I'll be back soon,' she said, kissing Allan's face.

'All right Sally. See you soon, Imogen,' he said.

Imogen stood behind Sally and stared at Allan without answering. Sally felt the walls closing in on her. There was no oxygen; she couldn't breathe. She noticed the silliest details: spiderwebs hanging from the ceiling, the light glinting from the eye of one of Ed's toy robots, his 'Best Effort' ribbon for a forward roll.

Nora drove and Sally hugged Imogen in the back seat of the car. She kept touching her forehead, checking for warmth. She was grateful to Nora for driving. If she had had to drive in this darkness she would have been stopping the car every ten minutes to check the road for dead bodies. As they pulled into the driveway Imogen began to talk in her sleep.

'Stupid Ed, Ed is dead.'

'Wake up darling, wake up. We're home,' said Sally.

'She's tired,' said Nora, opening the passenger door of the car.

Imogen stared back at Nora.

'Ed is stupid. Allan is not my dad, and Ed is not my brother.'

'Imogen, wake up,' said Sally.

'She doesn't know what she's saying. She's in shock. Let's get her inside,' said Nora.

After Sally had settled Imogen in bed, she sat at the kitchen table drinking tea from a delicate bone china cup and picking at a piece of Nora's latest cake creation, angel food cake.

'Terrible to lose a child this way,' said Nora.

Sally didn't know what to say. She felt too tired and too scared.

'I read about a gun accident like this last week. A boy in Huntly,' said Nora.

'Heartbreaking,' said Sally.

'Yes. A five-year-old boy shot his brother with a gun he found in a wardrobe.'

'People shouldn't leave loaded guns in wardrobes.'

'Poor Allan,' said Nora.

'He left the gun for a second. The police said it was an accident,' said Sally.

She rang Allan but he didn't answer. He must have gone to sleep. She undressed in the bathroom, and as she turned the shower tap

Imogen appeared in the doorway. Sally wrapped herself in a towel and bent over to Imogen's height.

'Imogen?' she said.

But Imogen's eyes were blank. She was sleepwalking.

'Ed is dead, Ed is dead,' she chanted.

'Imogen. Wake up, darling.'

Sally turned off the shower tap, led Imogen back to her bed and fell asleep next to her.

They returned to the farm early the next morning. Allan sat in the lounge in the low morning light. He looked at Sally and Imogen and lowered his head into his freckled hands. Someone had stacked Ed's toy tractors in the corner of the room next to a row of plastic toys – Spiderman, Superman, Spock, Lieutenant Uhura, Plastic Man, Brainiac.

'Why don't you go outside and play, Imogen?' Sally said.

Imogen ran from the room as the sunlight crept along the walls and revealed Allan's hollow face. Sally sank to the floor next to him and laid her head on his knees.

'Did you sleep?' she asked.

'Detective Crane rang. He's coming back this morning. He has more questions,' said Allan.

'What? I thought he'd finished with the questions.'

'There's some issue about the tests they did yesterday.'

They sat for a while listening to the weka calls.

'It was an accident, wasn't it? Imogen doesn't know how to shoot a gun. She's confused, and she was talking in her sleep,' said Sally.

'What's she saying?'

'I don't know. She's sleepwalking and sleep-talking; she's traumatised. She had the same reaction after her father died.'

Sally shuddered and remembered how Imogen had chanted in her sleep all those years ago, 'Daddy's dead, Daddy's dead.'

A melancholy shining cuckoo call echoed across the morning air from the two-hectare stand of kauri–broadleaf forest Allan had protected with a QEII covenant.

'Detective Crane said she should see a psychologist. He gave me this,' said Allan, handing Sally a pink and blue business card.

Sally read the card. 'Dr Haussen.'

She shuddered to think what a psychologist would uncover.

A police officer appeared at the door, a tall Māori woman with wide shoulders. She had the look of an athlete, and wore a heavy blue police jacket. Allan got up and helped Sally to her feet and they walked across the room to greet her. Allan stood with his arms hanging at odd angles by his sides. The police officer apologised with polite formality. She told them she needed to inspect the fence line, to take measurements with the officers from Forensics, and that Detective Crane was on his way.

'What's this all about?' said Sally.

'It's just routine: nothing to worry about. Detective Crane will be here shortly,' said the police officer.

'When can we have Ed back? We need to organise everything,' said Allan.

He dropped his head, and Sally reached for his hand.

'Detective Inspector Crane will be here in a few minutes. He can answer any of your questions,' the police officer said.

Sally nodded and watched her walk back to the police car parked in the driveway and speak to three other officers in plain clothes, lounging against the vehicles and smoking cigarettes. Allan slumped onto the sofa and sobbed, his body rounding into a tight knot. Sally sat next to him and put her hand on his back. A quick tear slid down her face and over her jaw.

'I'm so sorry, Allan.'

'I can't get Ed's face out of my head. There was so much blood. It was everywhere: all over Imogen, on the gun, Ed.'

His hands shook.

'Ed's eyes, his big blue eyes. The blood, Sally, the blood.'

He started to retch. He launched himself off the couch and ran out the door. Sally looked away through the ranchsliders to the covenanted bush. She could see the police officers walking along the fence line, pacing, measuring, taking photographs and writing on clipboards. After a while, Detective Crane appeared at the door and walked into the room.

'Good morning,' he said.

'Detective,' said Sally.

Allan emerged and stood in the hallway door, hugging his sides, his face pasty and drawn.

'Hello, Detective.'

'What's this all about?' said Sally again.

The detective wore another dark suit today.

'We've analysed the patterns of gunshot residue and blood, and we need to cover off a few areas of inquiry,' the detective said.

'What patterns?' said Sally.

'The patterns on Imogen's hands,' said the detective.

Sally and Allan followed Detective Crane out into the field. Imogen sat perched on the jungle gym in Allan's backyard, one knee hooked over the bar. She flung her body into a forward roll, looped around the bar into an upright position and flung herself around again, the tips of her long black hair grazing the grass as she spun. She steadied herself, with one leg hooked onto the bar, and faced the police officers walking along the fence line. A flock of geese flew overhead in V-shaped formation and disappeared over a hill. The cows hung their huge heads over the fence, large jaws chewing from side to side. Imogen brought both legs onto the bar and catapulted herself around into a backward flip dismount, landing on her feet in the grass, her arms outstretched in a finishing pose, her back arched. Black spangling gleamed on her top. She stood in mock triumph as Sally approached her with Allan and Detective Crane.

'That was an impressive somersault,' said Detective Crane.

Imogen stared at him.

'Detective Crane has some more questions to ask you, Imogen,' said Sally, reaching out a hand to her.

Allan stood close to Sally, his arm touching hers, his eyes wandering over the length of the fence line. Imogen clutched Sally's hand and looked at Detective Crane, waiting for him to speak.

'Imogen, can you tell me again what happened when the gun went off yesterday?' he said.

'Ed picked up the gun and I tried to take it off him.'

'So you both held onto the gun at the same time?'

'Ed was holding it and I tried to take it off him and he wouldn't let go.'

'Did you touch the gun first?'

'I don't know. He wouldn't let go,' said Imogen.

She began to cry, and looked up at Sally.

'All right, so you both held onto the gun – and then what happened?' said the detective.

'Go ahead, Imogen,' said Sally.

'I tried to take the gun away from him but he wouldn't let go, and then the gun went off and ...'

Allan turned his attention from the fence line to Imogen.

'Did you undo the safety lock, Imogen?' said the detective, pulling out a large brown envelope from the inside of his coat. He withdrew a photograph of a blood-spattered gun from it. 'This is the gun. Do you remember?'

Imogen nodded. Sally stifled a cry.

'See this red button?' The detective pointed at the picture. 'Did you see this button yesterday?'

'No,' said Imogen.

'No she didn't,' said Sally.

'Imogen. This is important,' said the detective.

'We were fighting over the gun, and I didn't see the red button,' said Imogen.

The wind got up in the covenanted bush, and the cows lowed in complaint. Allan stared at Imogen. Imogen stared at the detective. The detective stared back at her. Sally wondered if they could see the truth.

'I think we have all the information we need for now,' said the detective.

'Come on, Imogen. Let's go inside and make a cup of Milo,' said Sally.

Imogen let go of Sally's hand.

'I'm going to practise on the jungle gym,' she said, and ran away, looking back over her shoulder at the detective.

'Is something wrong, Detective?' said Sally.

'The gunshot residue patterns on the gun and on Imogen's hands are not what we expected. And there was no residue on Ed's hands,' said Detective Crane. He shook his head and said, 'It's unusual given the close range.'

'What are you saying? She tried to take the gun off him. They fought over it,' said Allan.

'You can appreciate we need to look at every angle. The blood splatter pattern ...' Detective Crane looked at Allan and said, 'I'm sorry about this.'

'No, I'm all right. What about the blood?' said Allan.

'There's no blood on Ed's hands. Not what we expected. At such close range … blood everywhere. The patterns we found suggested his hands may have been covered or held.'

'But their hands are so small,' said Sally.

Detective Crane gazed at Imogen playing on the jungle gym, and turned to Allan and Sally.

'We need to ask the questions, Miss Randerson. We have to put all the facts in front of the Coroner for the inquiry.'

Detective Crane nodded goodbye and walked over to the officers at the fence line. Allan and Sally stood in the long grass in the yard watching the police cars driving away from the farm. They stood there until the dust kicking up on the road had died down; until the sun beat down on their heads and the tūī hopping through the kōwhai trees began to scuffle with each other, their feathers flying. Until one shiny black bird sang out in victory.

Sally waited in the kitchen, expecting Ed to run through the door with grubby knees; expecting to hear his voice, his laughter. She jumped whenever the phone rang, whenever the purple tower leaves thonked against the window, whenever the wind blew. But still Ed did not return. She stood and walked to the door and then sat, stood and walked to the door and then sat, stood and walked to the door, expecting to see Ed playing with Imogen outside, and then sat. Allan's family stopped by the farm one by one to offer their condolences and to drop off braised stew and casserole and cake. His younger brothers, also farmers, had driven up to the farm in a battered old ute to help Allan milk the cows.

Allan took his brothers into the lounge to talk about Ed's funeral arrangements. By late afternoon everyone had left, and Sally stood at the kitchen sink drinking tea out of a Royal Albert teacup painted with old country roses. Imogen sat at the green Formica table drinking Milo and toying with a plate of red velvet cake from Nora. Nora and her cakes and her wedding dresses – her productions, she called them. Sally had asked Nora to bake their wedding cake. Nothing elaborate: just two tiers, with cherries and marzipan. But the cake would have to wait. The wedding would have to wait.

Sally watched Allan through the window walking back and forth across the grass, looking out towards the fence line. He had worked all summer to replace the fence. The old fence posts had lasted for fifty years: works of art, handmade from tōtara by Allan's grandfather. A relic from a bygone era.

Allan walked back into the kitchen and sat at the table.

'Why don't you try to get some sleep?' said Sally.

'I'm fine,' said Allan.

Imogen looked at Allan and said, 'How are we going to get the stains out of my leotard? My favourite one?'

'What?' he said.

'My black leotard! Ed's blood is all over it,' said Imogen.

She looked directly at Sally and said, 'I need it for next week.'

'Imogen, stop it. We'll wash it,' said Sally, tears forming in her eyes.

'Washing it won't work. It's my favourite, and he ruined it,' said Imogen.

'Imogen, you stop it right now! I know you don't mean it. You're upsetting your mother,' said Allan.

Red cake crumbs stuck to Imogen's fingers and face. She stopped chewing and sat looking at Allan.

'You are not my father, and when I get the chance ...'

Her face turned red. Sally clenched her fists.

'For God's sake, Imogen. Stop it!'

Imogen's face burned with fury as she continued spooning cake into her mouth. Sally felt a tight gripping sensation in her chest.

Allan got to his feet slowly and stared at Imogen, planting his hands on the table across from where she sat eating. Sally felt the hairs rise on the back of her neck, and a chill ran down her arms. Imogen lifted her chin and met Allan's gaze with unblinking defiance.

'I left that safety on; you know it,' he said.

He backed away from her and stumbled outside into the night. Sally ran after him into the cool settling air. They stood looking out to the fence line as the sun dipped behind the farm boundary. One star had risen in the sky. Sally wrapped her arms around herself.

'I put the safety lock on,' said Allan.

'Well, it must have worked itself loose or something,' said Sally.

Allan pushed his hands deep into his pockets. Sally shivered. The sun had begun its darkening descent behind the hills. She realised the marriage was not going to work. She would not find the freedom she sought with Allan, or ever. Imogen was too much like her, too much of a risk. Allan stood apart from her.

'I'm going to check the cows,' he said.

Sally watched his broad back as he walked away towards the field. Beyond him, the covenanted bush stood dark against the setting sun, a lone block of native flora preserved in perpetuity.

When Sally returned to the kitchen Imogen was dozing, her head resting on her arms on the table. There was no red velvet cake left on the plate, only a few red crumbs. The room looked dim and unwelcoming. Sally thought of Ed's little body alone in the morgue. She took the forks and plates from the table, rinsed them and arranged them in order in the dishwasher, the tines of the forks all facing the same way. At least she wouldn't see dead animals on the way home.

Baby Doll

I wish I have costume like Barbie. Her life so big life! We no have Barbie. We no have Barbie costume. But she have so much! She have own house, own pink car, own pink wardrobe la. Lucky I clock time card so early: 4.50 this morning. Bad story last Monday when I late on start time. They dock whole hour pay. No can lose so much money. No my fault I late. Big accident on cycle-way. Long time now, before I come many bike flow like silk ribbon in workshop when moon shine in morning. They all break bad. Nobody fix it. They take away scrap.

Now all girl walk in workshop in long line. I wait full moon make rice paddy like lamp. No moon shine last Monday. We walk on memory in dark. If you tire, if rock on path, if you new girl, la! You trip, you fall. If lucky you fall off cycle-way in soft rice paddy. Easy, you get up, carry on la. You fall on path? You hurt foot. Many girl fall and many girl hurt foot.

Last Monday one girl fall on path. I hear many scream, cry, splash. Many girl fall in rice paddy. I stop behind girl in front. I no fall in mud. We wait long time. We girl get back on path. Start moving. No girl hurt, thanks be la Allah. But ... I five minute late clock time card. I say my mother, 'They dock pay this month.' I think she sad.

Today I fill quota on Black Barbie President in America. I sit straight on seat, run material in machine, sew lapel on twenty pink jacket. I see Black Barbie President in America in pink jacket in three-quarter sleeve wave in crowd. I there. I, Black Queen in America, also wave in crowd in yellow jacket in three-quarter sleeve, yellow skirt. I laugh on best friend, Black Barbie President in America. One time I sew fifty jacket one run. I slow now. Pink everywhere, in air, in machine, in my hand. Material come straight in dye room. No dry, so wet. Smell in dye room catch in my throat every day. I want wash my throat kaow kaow. I want wear mask. One mask cost one week pay, no last long. Make buy, buy, buy. Pink dust catch in filter. You no breathe. Mask hot. Make pink line on mouth like you eat candy floss in market. Easy have no mask. Save one week pay, one week pay, one week pay.

My friend, she Hani girl from Yunnan Province on machine next row, orange scarf row. She big sick. Smell make girl sick we think. She go home. Girl go home ... no good. No come back. Hani girl – she die last week. We girl have sick. We girl know. Six month, cough start, you die. I start cough five month now when monsoon come, wash out cycle-way, we walk in mud. Rice worker make new cycle-way. I grateful la Allah I ten year old in three week. I want die ten year old. I girl child now, nine year old.

New girl from Sichuan Province, she now on Hani girl machine. She sew tiny pink on blue flower in Hawaii lei for Black Barbie President in America make vacation, on Honolulu. She sing on Hani girl machine. Machine cry first week, bad time. Machine make

Baby Doll

strange noise, wail-on-dead noise. Girl from Sichuan make go nicely la. Sing machine first week. For sure machine run smooth. You no sing dead girl machine? For sure break down la! No make quota. You no make quota. They dock pay. You wait repair man fix it. He busy fix other girl machine. Take long time. You sit round, round. No make quota. They dock pay.

Many girl sing in room. Big room. One hundred machine. Two shift. Sichuan girl rock side, side. She sew tiny Hawaii lei, she sing Sichuan love song. I know Sichuan love song now. She teach me. I sing my machine. One song I know. Uyghur lullaby my grandmother sing long time now. I sing Uyghur lullaby every day. Lullaby help me, I make quota first week. I put magic on machine. Machine run smooth now.

My back ache. One hour we go breakfast. Kanasai I want go toilet. Must wait toilet break. I, Black Queen in America? I want go toilet break? I go la! I sew fifteen pink lapel jacket on white rim stitch. I want work on next row. Red scarf row. Girl on red scarf row sew white tank top. Next row, blue scarf row sew flare skirt. Half hour go past quick. Girl from Sichuan Province sing, she look, look on machine. Baby pile little blue on white lei on table. So pretty. Next row, green scarf row, sew Hawaii grass skirt in straw, sew Māori grass skirt in same straw. Same skirt.

Māori Barbie she make tattoo on body. When I start sew long time now, I hurt finger and blood come out. I make tattoo with blood. Funny. No hurt finger now. Now I expert. I race on Sichuan girl. I sew ten jacket, she sew ten Hawaii lei. She sew ten Hawaii lei. I cough, cough long time. She win. Not fair.

Many sewing machine in room. Big noise in room. Needle go up down, up down – big noise. I hear girl sing. Sound terrible. No sing same song. Sound horrible. Many girl rock side, side. Sore muscle. We rock side, side like river. I dizzy. I tire. Same like summer time when monsoon cloud in sky, when wind blow girl on cycle-way. Summer time we work long night, fill quota. Last summer time I sew ski jacket Black Barbie President in America make ski vacation. Ski jacket silver on pink material. I sew diamond pattern on jacket. I want work next row with Sichuan girl, orange scarf row. She sew tiny pink ski mitten, so tiny like mouse ear. She try hard, Sichuan girl big fat finger. My finger good, fast. I want make pink ski mitten, tiny doll mitten. I sit wrong row, I sit white scarf row. Next row, red scarf row, sew fluffy collar on ski jacket. Next row, black scarf row, sew pink rib waist on pink ski pant. Next row, yellow scarf row, sew glitter pink fuzz on ski pant hem. Next row, I no see it. My eye red red sore.

One morning I wake up on mat in dormitory, I find tiny pink ski mitten in night dress. I share night dress on girl from night shift. She sew in next row, orange scarf row. Same row Sichuan girl sew pink ski mitten. Must be fall down la, get stuck on girl from night shift. What I do? I take ski mitten workshop? They dock my pay! I think, think fast fast. Fold night dress ready on girl in night shift. I think President! What she do? Queen? Hawaii Princess? Oh yes la! I keep it. Secret tiny pink ski mitten from Black Barbie President in America make ski vacation. I sew pink ski mitten inside hem my shirt. Nobody see it. Nobody know. I know.

She happy make ski vacation, Black Barbie President in America. She ski down tall mountain like mountain in Yunnan Province. Sichuan girl tell me she see mountain in Yunnan Province. I, Black Queen in America in fluffy yellow collar on silver jacket, in yellow ski pant. I ski down mountain loop, loop, loop. Huge snow fall on feet. Crazy snow, giant pattern. Snow pattern on plastic box on packing line. We ski, Black Barbie President in America, Princess Hawaii Barbie, Doctor Barbie. Doctor Barbie she fix my cough. We fall down mountain laugh, laugh, laugh.

Many girl my shift, we go breakfast break. We stand long line one cup rice, dry fish. I hungry oh. I think I want eat fried rice and Coke. I sit under mango tree. Many girl sit under mango tree. Girl from Sichuan Province rock side, side, eat, eat. We talk. Want make quota. Go home family. We eat slow make food go long way. Ten minute, end breakfast break. I see green mango hang on my head. I touch mango like belly, smooth, cool. My breath come slow, noisy like dragon roar in out, in out. I no here on mango gold, ready for eat. I no here.

Breakfast finish. I lean on machine, put head down on rest. I dream spring time. Rice high. Rice noisy in wind. My row, white scarf row, sew blue silk epaulette, Air Force One jacket. Tiny, tiny material we sew on gold. Many girl keep time like river. My row sew eight blue epaulette, red scarf row sew eight brass button, blue scarf row eight zipper, green row eight box pleat, purple row eight waist band, orange scarf row eight cuff. On, on, one girl faint. They dock girl pay. We stop few minute. Other girl go her seat. We start. One girl make sleep, sew finger. Blood fall on Barbie jacket. They dock girl pay. I like Air Force One jacket.

I, Black Queen in America jump out Air Force One. I wear yellow silk jacket, pink epaulette, pink helmet like Pop Up Parachute Barbie, free. No one stop me.

'Hey! Wake up Baby Doll!'

Girl from Sichuan Province shout at me. I wake up. Malaysian boss lady she high up la. Far away. She look like Malaysian Barbie. Perfect face. She no see me sleep, far away, no binocular, like Opera Barbie.

My row change. Now sew pink inauguration gown. I ask girl from Sichuan province what this mean 'inauguration'.

She say, 'You no work, no sew button on jacket, you take toilet break anytime. You Princess.'

This gown ... big work. I think Black Barbie President in America no like it. Inauguration gown so heavy so hot. Many frill. Neck so high, train so long like Princess Barbie wedding gown. I sew ten long train. I race Sichuan girl. She sew ten long white glove. I squeeze tiny pink ski mitten hide in hem. I see big life, many friend. We laugh. Best, best friend Black Barbie President in America make me Princess. Doctor Barbie she fix my cough. Pop Up Parachute Barbie she make me fly.

I dream my inauguration.

Ice

Bentley watched as Paris walked into the maths classroom, her shiny brown curls falling onto the curves of her face, a leather bag hanging off her tanned and smooth shoulder, and the bruise under her left eye a smudged, covered-over purple. The usual racket at the beginning of the day went quiet as Paris made her way to the group table and sat in the seat next to Bentley. After watching Warrant Officer Ripley kill the monster Alien, Sarah Bentley and her friends had taken to calling each other by their surnames: Bentley, Paris, Karunatilaka and Carmichael. Sophisticated and heroic, like Sigourney Weaver. Bentley wanted her surname to be what people thought of when they saw her, just like Ripley.

'He's gonna get it for what he did to you,' said Bentley.

'He didn't do it on purpose. I told you already,' said Paris.

'Paris loves the caretaker,' said Karunatilaka in a sing-song voice.

'I do not!'

Paris tugged at the navy blue ribbon in her hair and it came away in her hand. Her uniform looked brand new: the blue and white stripes and gold lion insignia shone bright and silken in comparison to the settled presentation of the other girls in the room, theirs washed and dry-cleaned into the dull tones of daily use.

'Love the hair,' she said, plumping her fingers into Bentley's short new hairstyle, desperate to change the subject.

'Thanks,' said Bentley.

Across the table, Carmichael and Karunatilaka resumed their banter about which one of them had scored highest in a science test. Bentley, Paris, Carmichael and Karunatilaka always placed in the top quartile – scholarship level and on their way to university degrees.

Paris removed the leather bag from her left shoulder and placed it on the floor next to her feet. The leather folded over, butting up against Bentley's leg, still warm from Paris's body. Moving away from this vicarious caress, Bentley went red in the face. Paris smiled at her as she crossed one leg over the other. She reached into her leather bag, took out a tablet covered in pink neoprene and placed it on the table. Her fingers, long and elegant with a clean French manicure, tapped at the tablet screen entering her passcode.

By the time Miss Roddenberry walked into the room, the familiar noise level of girls' voices and laughter had risen to a crescendo. She held up one large hand to call attention to herself, but it was hardly necessary. Miss Roddenberry possessed a commanding presence. She was almost two metres tall, with long curly red hair tied back into a ponytail.

'Quiet please. We are continuing today with simultaneous equations.'

Paris and Bentley rolled their eyes, mock yawned into their hands and then laughed when they began to actually yawn. A low rumbling groan emanated from the rest of the class.

'Please take out your tablets and go to the math lab wiki. You'll see I have set three exercises. Please work through them in your pairs. Post the solutions on the blog when you've finished and we'll go over them together.'

'Not again,' said Bentley.

'This won't take us long,' said Paris, tapping on her screen.

Bentley's black bag lay open on the table. She slid a hand inside with a practised movement and spun her tablet out and along the surface into a rotating arc. She had perfected this movement: the tablet would spin out and come to rest in front of her. The others had seen her perform this show countless times, and sometimes Paris would clap and laugh. Bentley enjoyed those days best of all. Nonchalant for Paris's benefit, she watched the tablet until it came to rest, and then folded back the fabric cover and placed it upright into the internal stand. She glanced over at Paris, who had missed the whole spectacle today. Miffed, Bentley put her head down into a sulk.

Across the table, Karunatilaka and Carmichael sat laughing behind their screens.

Tania Karunatilaka was one of three daughters of the Sri Lankan cultural attaché, and the genius in the group: she had the highest IQ of them all, and was top of the class in maths, digital technologies, earth and space science and chemistry. No one was surprised that she was the first person in the class to solve the formula pathway for exercise one. She peered over the shoulder of her best friend, Isabella Carmichael. They made an odd couple: Carmichael was tall and elegant, with straight blonde hair and translucent white skin. She looked like a super model or a champion tennis player. Karunatilaka stood two heads shorter and already looked professorial, with a serious cast to her face behind her large black-framed glasses. They lived next door to each other in the diplomatic quarter on the cliffs of St Heliers, and drove to school together in a white two-seater sports car belonging to Karunatilaka: a gift from her parents. They were a mysterious pair in their little car, Karunatilaka childlike, straining to see over the steering wheel, while Carmichael's Danish head scraped the interior of the convertible roof.

Bentley worked out the equations with Paris. Although she would make certain allowances for Paris's fragile state, Bentley also wanted to make sure Paris kept up with them, for her own good. Bentley saw the other two had finished exercise one and posted it to the blog, and had begun working on exercise two. The blog entries confirmed the names of the few girls at other tables in the room who could usually keep up with them. Miss Roddenberry stood at the front of the class helping the girls who struggled with the formulas, demonstrating calculations on the whiteboard. Bentley gazed at Paris, oblivious to anything around her as she tapped on her tablet.

'Is your father back from Antarctica yet?'

'No,' said Paris, frowning at her screen. 'He won't be back for months. He loves it there with his telescopes and his cameras.'

'What does your mother say?' said Carmichael.

'She doesn't care. They like it this way. And Mum has her boyfriend, John,' said Paris, a sneer on her face.

They had all heard from Paris about her parents' separation. They'd each received the late night calls, the instant messaging, the FaceTiming from Paris in tears.

'Is John still hanging around?' said Bentley.

Paris nodded her head and said nothing more.

'Oh,' said Bentley, raising her eyebrows and leaning onto her elbows as she cast her eyes around the table at the others.

Paris hung her head and tapped her fingernails against themselves. She asked Bentley for the next code as she made her way through each step of the equation. She laughed when Bentley's large fingers hit the number nine key instead of the number eight. The mistake sent the graph lines off to the left of her screen in a warped tangent of jagged peaks and catenary arches. Bentley corrected the error. The pink and blue graph lines danced and transformed and resolved themselves into the correct parabolic curve. Bentley smiled and said they had cracked it. Paris agreed, and they uploaded the solution for exercise two.

'I can already see the answer to exercise three,' said Bentley, yawning.

'Can you keep a secret?' said Paris to the group.

'What secret?' said Bentley.

'Yeah, what?' said Karunatilaka.

'I'm meeting him in the bell tower later.'

'Are you nuts? After what he did to you?' said Bentley.

Paris touched the bruise under her eye. 'I need you to keep watch,' she said.

Tipping her chair on its two back legs, Bentley folded her arms and balanced.

'Why are you hanging out with a meth head?' said Karunatilaka.

'Yeah,' said Carmichael, nodding her head. 'I mean, I know he's fit and muscly, but he gave you a black eye.'

Paris sat with one limp arm hanging over the edge of the blue shimmer surface, the other arm propped under her chin. Her white blouse draped open, revealing a pink sports bra, tight against tanned skin.

'I told you. He didn't mean to do it. He danced around me and I didn't watch where I was going and I got in his way.'

'Yeah, dancing on meth,' said Bentley.

'He's not evil. Look, I want to see him one more time to tell him it's over,' said Paris.

No one spoke.

'Please?'

'Well, it has to be the last time,' said Bentley.

'Thank you,' said Paris, hugging Bentley, who flushed pink in the face and on her chest through her shirt.

At the end of the maths class the group crowded together and shuffled out of the room.

'Where are we going now?' said Paris.

'To the science lab: follow me,' said Bentley.

Paris fell in behind and became wedged between Karunatilaka and Carmichael. The hallways were crowded with chattering girls moving in a heaving mass from one class to the next. A familiar transitional din bounced off the concrete pillars and shiny timber walls. The echoing sound of the girls in this part of the building always reminded Bentley of a flock of seagulls screaming into the wind. Carmichael jammed up against Bentley and looped an arm over her elbow.

'What do you think?' she said, cutting her blue eyes back towards Paris.

'Not good. We'll sort it over recess,' said Bentley.

Gripping Bentley's arm tighter, Carmichael pushed into the backs of other girls as the crowd thickened into a bottleneck at the end of the hall. The front girls forced a path through the doorway and out to a landing on the other side, where the stream released into a delta. Half of them poured downstairs to the music suite and the other half walked to a sky bridge arching over to the science block. Above the squawking seagull noise, Bentley heard Paris's voice behind her, talking to Karunatilaka. She hoped Paris was talking about something other than the assistant caretaker. Anybody might hear her in this jam. Through the glass walls of the sky bridge, they had a clear view between two brick buildings of the northern slopes of the school gardens, where the assistant caretaker operated a leaf blower in methodical sweeping movements. Carmichael pulled up short with Bentley and they stood and watched him. They could also see a group of girls stopped on the path next to him, bunching around one girl who was bending over and taking an inordinate amount of time to tie her shoelaces. They could see him watching the girls watching him, his light brown hair sticking out at rakish angles from under large ear protectors. He wore the same outfit every day: shorts, gaiters, T-shirt, boots. Bentley found this at once hideous and fascinating. She had always remarked upon it to Paris, who in turn contended he was not dirty, just poor.

The four of them crowded into each other, forming a huddle at the apex of the glassed-in sky bridge. A continuing stream of girls flowed around them like blood cells rushing past a bulging plaque obstruction in the wall of an artery. Standing still, observing him, the group took a collective in-breath as he stopped and turned and looked in their direction. Bentley doubted that he could see them from so far away in the garden, but it was uncanny that he had looked up at that particular moment. He paused.

'Oh, he can see me,' said Paris, pulling in behind Bentley.

'Impossible at this distance,' said Karunatilaka, and they knew it to be true coming from her. She had demonstrated on many occasions an ability to calculate spatial distance with total accuracy, the gaps between objects a source of unending obsession for her.

'What is he doing?' said Carmichael, her face pressed up against the glass.

Paris groaned and tried to drag Carmichael away.

'Whatever he's doing doesn't matter because he's a nobody,' said Bentley.

'Come on,' said Paris, walking away.

They unpacked onto the long tables in the science lab and sat in bunched-up pairs next to the Bunsen burners. Bentley sat next to Paris and stared at the bald man at the front of the room, Mr Booth. As always, Karunatilaka sat with Carmichael. Having posted written instructions on the large screen, Mr Booth, a lanky Englishman, walked along the rows and handed out Petri dishes and spoonfuls of blue and white chemicals for the experiment. The girls babbled as he made his way along the benches and back to the front of the room, where he waited and watched. He didn't have the same control of the girls as the other teachers. Clapping his hands trying to get the class to be quiet and failing, he shouted over their heads in a thick Geordie accent.

'Will you SHUT UP?' He banged on the wall heartily with his fist, and tried to give them instructions for the next step in the experiment.

His desperation only served to make the whole room erupt into raucous laughter. Red-faced and anxious, Mr Booth banged on the wall again and again until the laughter subsided.

'So, when are you meeting him?' said Bentley.

'After morning recess,' said Paris.

'Oh? And why at the bell tower?'

Paris smiled and applied clear gloss to her perfect lips.

'The bell tower is our place, where he first ... you know ... kissed me,' she said, and flicked her hair back.

Paris stayed quiet during the rest of the science lab and didn't want to handle any of the chemicals, even though she wore the necessary hot mitts. She wouldn't handle the pipettes or the tongs or any of the beakers. Nor would she ignite the burner, a nothing task Bentley thought might be easy for her.

'It's okay. You can touch the stuff. You've got gloves on,' said Bentley, as she lifted a spoonful of shiny blue crystals into a beaker to demonstrate.

Paris would have none of it. She refused to participate in any way with the experiment, her mouth set as if she could explode at any minute. Bentley looked wide-eyed at Karunatilaka and Carmichael, and shrugged. For the rest of the lesson Paris sat perched on a stool in her hot mitts and safety goggles and watched them.

With a tense smile, Mr Booth patrolled the room, his hands clasped behind his back. His eyes flicked back and forth over each of the outlet stations as he tried in vain to retain a face of patient good humour. Chemicals bubbled in beakers around the room and crystals formed as the girls turned off the Bunsen flames and the class drew to a close.

At morning recess, the group made their way to a sunny spot on the front lawn. Spreading their bags out on the grass, they cast a Wiccan semicircle to the sun as they waited for the assistant caretaker to appear. Right on cue, as if summoned by magic, he emerged from behind one of the rhododendron bushes, raking and pruning and moving along the line of pink and purple flower heads. He shot a furtive glance at the group, and Paris smiled back at him.

'He's revolting,' said Bentley.

Paris pretended not to hear. She dragged her fingers through her hair, curved her neck into a magazine pose and smiled again.

'I bet he's on meth right now,' said Bentley.

'No he's not.'

'Paris, you are in love with an assistant caretaker who smokes meth,' said Bentley.

'No I'm not. I'm breaking up with him. Look, it's me. I'm the one who smokes the meth, all right? Not him.'

She blushed, applied lip gloss to her bow-shaped lips and flipped her hair out of her eyes with an upward head twist.

'What the hell are you talking about?' said Bentley.

Paris glared at her. 'John gives it to me,' she said.

'You're kidding ...' said Carmichael, looking around at the group wide-eyed. 'Meth will rot your brain.'

'What a mess,' said Karunatilaka, shaking her head.

Paris tossed her mane, and looked over at the assistant caretaker to see if he was looking. He continued raking leaves and smiled at her. Then he threw the rake into the wheelbarrow and grabbed both handles. Pushing the wheelbarrow in front of him, he walked in slow methodical steps and paused in the middle of the lawn right in front of them.

'What's wrong with you lot?' he said, pointing at them with his chin.

'Do your work,' said Bentley.

'Shut up,' said the caretaker.

'So rude. *You* shut up, or we'll report you. You idiot,' said Bentley.

They all laughed except for Paris, who looked sad. The assistant caretaker picked up speed. His face turned a burning shade of crimson and he skulked and arched his shoulders, the impressive muscles of his thighs working in lockstep as he wheeled the barrow away.

'Stick a pineapple up your bum sideways,' he said in a final parting shot before he disappeared from view of the group.

'Classy. Dickhead!' said Bentley.

'Sarah!' Paris feigned horror.

'Emma!' said Bentley, in a teasing voice.

The group laughed as the assistant caretaker retreated. Bentley turned to Paris.

'So what happens? You go up into the bell tower and smoke meth with him? Did you go up there yesterday?'

'Yeah.'

'Disgusting. So what are you going to do up there today?' said Karunatilaka.

They stared at Paris. She preened and laughed and tried to act like a queen holding court. 'Mum doesn't know about John giving me ice. And I don't want to smoke it any more. I'm going to tell Brock it's over,' said Paris.

'Is that his name: Brock? Are you serious?' said Bentley.

'Look, it's okay. I just started mucking about with him, and now he's into it. But it's got to stop. I know that. And I have to stop too. Please help me with this.'

Paris's words resonated in the air, repeating in their ears.

'So what do you want us to do?' said Karunatilaka.

'I need one of you to stand watch at the bottom of the stairs while I go up and talk to him in the bell tower,' said Paris.

'Why the bell tower? Why now?' said Bentley.

'I told you why. He'd be suspicious if I suggested anywhere else, and I have to do this now. I'll go crazy if I don't do something,' said Paris.

They watched the caretaker on the far side of the lawn tending the rhododendrons, pruning and raking. Karunatilaka and Carmichael exchanged a look.

'Our next class is earth and space science. Miss Clarke saw us this morning at assembly. We can't cut class,' said Carmichael.

They turned to Bentley.

'I've got English with Miss Soane.'

'Come on, please,' said Paris.

Bentley lay back on the grass and watched the caretaker as he raked the leaves.

'Okay. I'll handle it.'

They leaned back into the sunshine like a pod of basking seals until the bell buzzed in the main building and they roused themselves out of their heated stupor.

'What have you got next, Paris?' said Bentley.

'I'm going to study in the library. So there's no problem.'

'What should I do? What if someone sees me?' said Bentley.

'Hide behind the pillars. No one will see you. I think there's a cleaning cupboard. I just need someone to be a lookout and to help me if something happens.'

'Like what?' said Bentley.

'I don't know what,' said Paris, her eyes pleading.

'We better go,' said Karunatilaka, and she grabbed Carmichael's hand and helped her up.

They stood over Paris, casting her into partial shadow. Paris held her arm up, shielding her eyes from the sun.

'Take care,' said Carmichael.

Karunatilaka pulled her away.

'See you at lunchtime,' said Paris.

Bentley helped Paris stand up and they swayed into each other, groggy from too much sun.

'All right. I'll be there soon, okay?' said Bentley.

Paris nodded, and jogged away across the lawn in the direction of the library. She turned and ran backwards, and Bentley stood and watched her brown curls bobbing and tangling over her face as she waved at Bentley and then turned around again. Bentley looked for the caretaker, but couldn't see him.

The Year 13 common room looked empty except for a few of the hockey girls sitting in the corner and Geraldine Bale sitting by the window reading.

'Geraldine, are you going to English?' said Bentley.

Geraldine looked up from her book. 'Yep, I'm going now. Are you coming?'

Bentley clutched at her stomach and screwed her face up in pain. 'I'm cramping real bad and I'm flooding. Can you tell Miss Soane I'm going to be late?'

'Of course. Go to the sickbay,' said Geraldine.

Bentley rushed out of the room and ran up to the landing near the staircase leading to the bell tower. She tried the door to the staircase, but couldn't open it. Paris must have a key, she thought. She felt exposed on the landing, and the pillars wouldn't hide anything.

The door to the cleaning cupboard was unlocked. The interior looked dark and dusty. She could see a few dirty mops leaning in a corner, a metal bucket in the middle of the floor and plastic bottles filled with pink fluid lined up along the timber walls. She stepped in and closed the old wooden door. The enclosed darkness reeked of stale chemicals. Daylight shone around the edges of the doorway. She upended the bucket and sat looking through an antique brass keyhole, hoping no one would find her.

Bentley was the writer in the group. With the encouragement of Miss Soane, she had won two secondary school literary competitions. She thought of her latest homework exercise, on 'drama and characterisation'. She wondered if she could use this drama in her writing. Paris would be the main character. People were playthings for Paris: trapped in her hypnotic gaze, people would willingly die for her, as though they had discovered their fate, their duty. Paris wanted a medical career. What particular aspect of medicine she didn't know, but some area of medicine would receive her brilliance, and she would leave a trail of bodies in her ethereal wake. Paris waited like a praying mantis for someone in her orbit with programmed DNA willing to sacrifice themselves to the higher good, the continuation of their genus: to never question their fate but to submit to her crazy damaged beauty.

Through the keyhole Bentley saw a Year 9 student trip and fall over on the wooden floor in the corridor. The caretaker stood right there. He bent and helped the young girl up.

'Are you all right?' he said.

The young girl cried into the back of her hand.

'Yes, thank you,' she said, and ran away from him.

Bentley held her breath and restrained herself from coughing. He was standing next to the cupboard, his hands twitching by his sides. She thought he might open the door and find her crouching on the metal bucket. But he moved away, his gaiters rubbing together and making a scraping noise. Bentley wondered how long this bell tower scene would take, and leaned back against the mops and the plastic bottles. The chemical smell and the warm enclosed space made her feel sleepy.

When the lunch bell buzzed, Bentley was shocked awake from a slumped-over position. She looked around in the darkness, confused and disoriented, until she saw a crack of light under the door and remembered she had shut herself in a cupboard. She heard the seagull clamour of the entire school on the move to lunch break. The pitch sounded strange from where she sat on the bucket: more screechy and insistent. As she listened, the door of the cupboard flew open. She fell off the bucket and it tipped over, making a concatenation of metallic clanging sounds, as the mops and plastic bottles dropped on her head. Paris stood framed in the doorway, a look of panic on her face.

'What the fuck, Paris!' said Bentley, untangling herself and clambering out of the stuffy cupboard.

Paris looked out of breath, confused, frightened.

'Come ... come ... quick ... he ... he ...'

'What's going on?'

'He's gone mad.'

'Calm down. What happened?'

Bentley grabbed Paris by the shoulders and shoved her behind the pillars. 'Breathe. Tell me what happened.'

Paris was sweaty and twitching uncontrollably.

'Look! Get a grip. What's going on?' said Bentley.

'We ... we ... we smoked some meth.'

'No!'

'I stole a bit of John's secret stash for our last hit together.' Paris pulled Bentley toward the stairs. 'He keeps saying he's going to fly and he ... he wouldn't get off the ledge. Quick ... Quick.'

'Hang on, calm down,' said Bentley.

Paris's pupils were fully dilated, like dark pools of chilled cave water.

'No one saw you go into the bell tower, right?' said Bentley.

'I don't know. Quick, he's going to jump!'

'Paris, did you leave anything up there with him?'

'No. I ran. I ran when he started going nuts. Please, you have to help.'

Bentley grabbed the lapels of Paris's jacket and shook her. 'Paris, control yourself. Come with me. We're going out to the lawn.'

'No. We can't.'

Pulling her towards the lawn, Bentley said, 'Get a grip. You're high. If you get caught like this you'll be suspended. What about your career? You won't get into med school. You don't want anything to do with this. Come on.'

As they left the building, the seagull noise had turned into screaming. The whole school could have been on the front lawn. Bentley held tightly onto Paris's hand and hauled her into the crowd of girls to where the others stood waiting. Karunatilaka and Carmichael stood huddled together in a hug, looking up at the bell tower. Bentley turned and saw the caretaker standing on the ledge with his arms outstretched and his head thrown back. Paris stared up at him in a frozen drugged-out haze. Bentley could see girls moving in the windows of classrooms under the bell tower, oblivious to the event taking place above them. Many girls walked along the footpath below, also unaware.

The caretaker floated in slow motion into a perfect swan dive. He hovered in the air. Now he looked like Wile E Coyote when Road Runner tricks him and he runs over the ledge of the Grand Canyon before he realises he is in mid-air and then plummets. A navy blue ribbon floated free of his hand and spiralled into the sky. Paris stared numb. Some girls shrieked and gasped, and some stood paralysed and silent as he fell. Bentley didn't see him hit the ground, but she heard a thud followed by a swell of screams emanating from the front of the crowd and travelling back to her in an oscillated wave of sound. And then they ran. They ran helter-skelter like frightened birds. Bentley stood unmoving as the crowd scattered. She stirred only when she realised she could see Paris running towards the caretaker. She ran after her and stopped in the confused mass of girls as Paris changed course and ran to a rhododendron bush.

'What are you doing?' said Bentley as she caught up to her.

Paris reached up on her tiptoes and removed a navy blue ribbon from a large mauve flower head.

'My ribbon,' she said, rubbing it against her cheek.

'Come on,' said Bentley, grabbing Paris's arm.

A few girls stood crying at a distance from the assistant caretaker's body as he lay unmoving on the grass. Bentley took Paris by the shoulders and manoeuvred her away and out of sight of him. As they passed by she glanced over and saw his face bloodied and white in a death stare. Paris looked over her shoulder at him, but Bentley pulled her away.

Later in the day when Bentley went to find her friends they had all gone, lost in the aftermath. The school had closed early, and the girls had all gone home. The police had seized tablets and mobile phones from many of the girls in the crowd who had filmed the assistant caretaker falling. Or jumping? Or diving?

Paris's mother had picked her up and whisked her away, and Karunatilaka and Carmichael fled in the white sports car.

Bentley knew there would be no consequences for any of them. The police would not link Paris with the caretaker. They would all be offered grief counselling, the same as when one of their teachers died in a car accident the previous year.

Bentley sat on the lawn trying to disappear into a large rhododendron bush, hoping it would envelop her as she waited for her mother to pick her up. As the sun shone into her face she sensed a slight movement in the leaves of the rhododendron bush, and she leaned over to look. There, gripped onto a leaf as wide as a sheet of paper, stood a single praying mantis.

At first, she had not seen the well-camouflaged insect: a delicate creature the identical green colour of the leaf upon which it stood poised. The tiny triangular head swivelled to look at her with bulbous eyes. She could see that its belly was swollen with eggs. It rocked back and forth on spindly legs in a crazy swing dance motion, as though surfing the leaf on currents of air. It looked Bentley square in the face, its antennae waving in lazy circles, mesmerising her. The monstrous little head rotated as if cocking an ear in conversation. Receiving no answer, it turned and scampered off into the leaves.

Grain Stacks

My life is always falling on the ground and breaking apart. Six months ago, at the age of nineteen years, I decided to stop looking at the broken pieces and began to look at the impressions they made in the dirt. I thought about this each day as we passed the roadworks on Great North Road. At first, I tried to stay in place, setting my foundations along the road. At first, I thought about it as just an old road; nothing about it moved me. Background light flickered into my eyes as I leaned my head against the smudged window of my father's dirty old four-wheel drive. He called it his 'truck', but it was a rickety rusty heap with huge tyres. The truck felt like our other home. We were always going places in it. I would study the back of my mother's head as she sat quietly in front of me looking straight ahead, her long black hair drawn onto the top of her skull in ropey coils. My father's knotted hands, driving, never leaving the steering wheel. Racheli my sister on the seat next to me looking out the window, her eyes dreamy, unfocused. Day after day we drove along Great North Road, past the houses and the people with their gardens and their driveways and their cars. The road stayed put, dependable. Nothing changed on the road except the light and the weather, until the day I saw the empty house.

My favourite snatches of time on the road I hold in my mind, in catalogue. Such fleeting moments. Favourite number one – a morning in autumn as the sun hit a long row of tall concrete barriers, turning them into rippling molten slabs. A surprising queue of huge blocks standing side by side, boiling gold alien beacons. I tried to hold onto the golden light in my mind and it has remained, imprinted, but it's elusive and I have to concentrate in the recall. I have looked for this phenomenon since I first encountered it, but I haven't seen it happen again with such emphatic clarity – although one time came close in a muted and less spectacular version. This is my all-time favourite. The light unique to the conditions, to the air, to the slant of the sun. Lasting for a blazing moment before we moved past it and I found myself back in the truck, back in a world of corrugated grey.

Favourite number two – a morning in early winter. The sky cast a brilliant red burn over everything. I can't describe it as unearthly because was it spread out around us, the sun a low rhubarb dot above the early urban haze, visible in strobes between the trees and the buildings. The entire sky blazed in gradations of red to rose pink. The light held and threw a blood hue into the interior of the truck. My father's eyebrows looked black beneath a devil-red forehead, my mother's black hair a red silhouette of magimagi thick as cod line. In the corner, my sister a coral glow, melding into momentary pink leather. I knew she loved it too. I wanted the world to remain swathed in eerie red light, warm, suspended in time.

Favourites number three, four and five: (three) Anytime it rains in full sheeting planes with angles and dullness and ancient hues and tinges of watery blue and purple; (four) Rainbows, because I know they form a perfect circle of perfect colour; (five) Anytime there's a rolling fog and the air is so thick with mist we must slow to a blind white stop. End of line.

Anyway, as I said, six months ago it all changed. A transformation began on the stretch of road across from the BP station where I noticed an empty house with no curtains. The light shone clear through, from one side of the house to the other. Nothing remarkable, nothing to be alarmed about, I thought. Someone had moved out, no cause for panic, and someone else would move in and put up new curtains to corner the light. But day after day, the house remained empty. Then another house emptied, and another. In a constant run, house after house emptied out until there was a whole block of see-through houses, stranded, mysterious, unexplained. I wondered if the houses belonged to the state and the corporation had ordered a renovation, a modernisation. Huge black spray-painted numbers began to appear on the front of each vacant house. Chain link fences covered in green fabric sprang up, shutting off the houses from the road and shading them from view unless you were stopped in the traffic or stood looking from the BP station across the road or sat in a rusty old truck, high above the other vehicles, like we did. The empty houses behind the chain link fence began to disintegrate, in slow methodical breakdown. It made me think of cracked pack ice floating away in a big thaw. I had seen a big thaw on TV once, in a documentary about frozen rivers, on a day when I stayed home from school. The rivers freeze over on the surface but continue to flow underneath until the earth shifts on its axis and the sun arrives and the ice sheet cracks and breaks into chunks and flows downstream.

First, the machines ripped open the outer cladding of each house, revealing wooden studs and dusty old pink GIB board. Next, a bulldozer appeared, tearing at framework, breaking the houses apart, leaving piles of rubble and nothing else. Two stalwart inhabitants hung on to the last minute, until one morning I saw them scrambling to fill a trailer as their neighbour's house was destroyed by a wrecking John Deere.

After the first row of houses disappeared, a second row, hidden from the road, was revealed. These houses too were broken down into rubble. A row of houses way in the back stood untouched for so long I hoped they would stay. But one day we drove past and they had gone too. A cleared space remained: a bald patch of land. I wanted to say to the men in the bulldozers, 'You forgot the ripped magazine over there, and the dirty running shoe in the corner, and the dusty teddy bear near the back fence line.' But they walked past those forgotten treasures. They cleared away the flowers, cut down the trees and pulled out shrubbery. One beautiful piece of vegetation remained for a while, a single bird of paradise, holding its bird heads high, sprouting orange and blue inflorescence and smoky green spathe. But in time, it too disappeared. I hope it was taken to live in the hothouse at the Domain. The site where it had grown was laid bare. Each morning I sank back into my seat as we approached the site, wary of the changing spectacle.

I did not expect what happened next. The men in orange vests started to construct a new building in the corner of the site. They made a new road for their heavy trucks complete with traffic lights, an office with metal grills on the windows, a car park for the site workers and a covered area with picnic tables. A new contained world arose, a secret fenced-in world with men in orange overalls rushing from the

Grain Stacks

BP station and stuffing meat pies into their mouths, security guards pacing importantly at each gate, ominous barbed wire and military style gatehouses.

Three cranes appeared in the skyline, yellow, grey and blue. Then a fourth one arrived in red. In the end I think there were six cranes, spread out over the site. As we drove by each day I tried to count them. But it was tricky because they moved about and criss-crossed in the sky as we drove past. I looked forward to seeing them in conversation with each other, their spindly bodies and steepled heads nodding back and forth. They reminded me of the Spirograph set at my primary school, with the gearwheels one inside the other and my pen spinning round and round creating geometric shapes. Some days the cranes sat clear in the light in chiefly huddles, their individual colours on display to full effect. Other days they were dark and swivelling, hard at work, and I couldn't tell red from grey, yellow from blue. On those shadowy days they were busy pieces of machinery and did not wish to be interrupted. Whole herds of other heavy machinery lumbered about the site, tractors and bulldozers and trucks, rigs and lines and shackles. I saw a strange new world. And that is what I craved.

My parents didn't talk about the road. They didn't talk about anything much at all. My father would order my mother about and complain if she didn't put his meals on the table in time. Apart from barking orders, he didn't talk to her. My mother would sometimes whisper to me and my sister to hurry and put on our good dresses for church, or hurry to the table, or play in silence. We had to be quiet near my father, especially inside the truck. He said he needed to concentrate when he was driving and he didn't want any noise distracting him. If there were roadworks, we were to be still while he slowed with the rest of the traffic, turning his head from side to side trying to see what had happened.

The construction site grew in place for six months: the exciting new landscape across the road from the BP station. I could no longer remember what the houses looked like. I couldn't hold onto them in my mind. The world of houses had vanished, supplanted by this new monstrous scene.

My father drove straight on as usual. My mother remained in her seat, unmoved. Her head did not turn to look. While I could no longer remember the houses, I remembered giving in as the machines destroyed them. I closed my eyes as we drove past and tried to disappear into the back seat. I had learned this trick early on. It all went back to an ending that was thrust upon me when I was five years old. The day of dark shadows at church camp, when I saw my father punch my mother in the face while she held my baby sister. I felt her grip my hand, and then she let go as she fell straight over onto her back in slow motion, clutching Racheli the whole way. Blood burst out from her nose. If I had only held onto her hand. That ended something for me. I would run behind my mother whenever he drew near. I felt unable to play with other children, fearful of leaving her side. Then one day my turn came, and he thumped me on the back.

The beginning of school marked the end of my time alone with my mother and my sister. They had to sit in the truck with me while my father drove me to school. He drove me to school every day, except for one time. That was the day I mentioned – then, he made me stay home from school because I had another bruise. This time it was on my chin, swollen and blue in plain view. My mother cried and hugged me and made me a cup of Milo. Then she went to sleep. I sat on the couch for hours, watching TV, frozen on the surface like a frozen river and coursing underneath.

Grain Stacks

My parents didn't fuss as Racheli and I stepped out of the truck at school. Our mother smiled from the window as the truck pulled away, and Racheli and I stood waving from the footpath. In heated classrooms, I would cross my legs under the desk, prop my head on my hands, and float away outside the window. My teachers would clap and call my name. They would walk over to me and squat down to my level as I sat at my table. Then I would see them. They made me go to the clinic for eye checks and ear tests. But I had perfect sight and excellent hearing. I could see even the smallest nuance of light, and my hearing was so finely tuned that I sometimes had to put my hands over my ears if life became too loud. I was assigned a teacher aide. She smelled of mouldy grass as she leaned across the desk and taught me the alphabet and numbers. I remember she made me write the letter O over and over again. My hand went round and round in the same place, and I dug the pencil deep into the paper until a deckle-edged O dropped out. A raggedy black sun. I glued it onto a sheet of white paper and surrounded it with crayon grey clouds. The teacher aide told me my black sun picture made her sad and reminded her of Monet. I thought she said 'money', like a fifty-cent piece. But she said, 'No, Monet, a French painter.' While she did not explain what 'French' meant, or 'painter', I understood that sunlight could be sad. My mother looked sad. After school, my father would be waiting in the truck outside the school gates, with my sunlit mother.

Sometimes we would go to pray at Pastor Uncle Levi's house. My Uncle Levi is the pastor of our church. We would go to church several times a week and on Sundays. My father drove us in the truck. We spent so much time in the truck, in silence. I would listen to the rhythm of the rattling windows and watch the sagging roof upholstery pulsing as the engine idled at red traffic lights.

The windows turned into prison bars, and my sister and I would hunch our shoulders over like convicts hiding our faces from the outside world until our father turned us over to the custody of teachers or Pastor Uncle Levi. My mother and my sister and I are my father's prisoners. He drives us everywhere we need to go: home, school, church, supermarket, superclinic. Sometimes on Saturdays we go to the shopping mall, but we have to be there before 2.55 p.m. so my father can watch the races at the TAB.

Six months ago, at the time the houses started disappearing, my father started driving me to university. He drove me to the Arts building in the morning and deposited me on the side of the road, where I entered the throng of students, and in the afternoon he picked me up at the same spot with my mother sitting in the front of the truck and my sister in the back seat, dreaming her dreams out the window. My father and my Pastor Uncle Levi were strict about education. I was the first person in my family to go to university, and they prayed for my success.

I tried to stay in place, to attend lectures, tutorials. But no one watched me at university. No teachers clapped in my face. Crowds of people crushed into me, and I navigated it all on my own. Lucky for me, my father had no idea how this works. He didn't have much education, hadn't been to university. As a boy he worked in the kaivalagi copra plantations on Kanacea Island in Fiji, with his cousins, husking coconuts and thatching the roofs of village bures. He didn't understand that high school is different to university. I had to provide him with a note from one of the lecturers to prove I had lectures at night. After the night lectures he would sit in the truck waiting for me in the darkness with my mother and my sister.

Every day driving past the roadworks across from the BP station and into town to the same spot outside the Arts Faculty. Every day standing on the kerb waving to my mother. Every day attending lectures. I attended lectures for a while. My favourites: 'Fine Arts 103: Drawing and Related Practices', 'French 101: Introductory French Language' and 'Art History 109: Shock of the Modern: Monet to Warhol'. I couldn't forget Claude Monet, the way he painted one cathedral over and over as the light shifted: in morning light, morning sun, morning effect, in grey, in pink, in sunlight, in grey weather, in dull weather, in gold. The way he painted grain stacks over and over: at the end of summer, in mid-winter with snow on top, at sunset, in white frost, in the morning, at midday, on a foggy morning, in the mist. The way he painted frozen rivers over and over: frozen white with colour bleeding through everywhere waiting to be released in the big thaw; with white ice floes in thaw floating on black water under a black-mauve sky; with ice floes adrift in cool pale yellow light beneath the ridge of a hill shimmering in delicate lilac and violet; with ice floes at twilight in water glowing rusty red butting up against orange riverbanks. The way he woke up in the morning and went to the same spot and painted the same thing, over and over. The way he caught the light, the fact he wanted to catch the light. I knew what he meant.

The day my formal education ended began in the same way as each day before it. As usual, my father dropped me off at the kerb outside the Arts Faculty. I was supposed to attend a lecture on Édouard Manet, but I didn't make it. As I said, I couldn't forget Monet, and how he didn't follow other painters who sat in the Louvre and copied the old masters, how he would go into the world and paint what he saw, his obsession with going to the same place multiple times.

His obsession became my obsession, and it freed me from my prison. It was freedom to know you could choose to go to one place over and over and watch the light and record it and forget everyone else.

This particular morning, my mother was not well. She should have been in bed resting. But he made her come with us. The air was bright. As I walked towards the lecture theatre I caught sight of a girl from church, Creola. She's studying for a degree in town planning. She told me she had to go to the library to get some books, and said I should cut my Manet lecture and go with her and we could check out the hacky-sacking boys by the fountain in Albert Park. So I did. She asked me how things were going. I told her how we got stuck in traffic every day near the construction site opposite the BP station. She knew about it already. She told me it's going to be a tunnel road to link the southern motorway with the western motorway, closing the Western Ring Route. She showed me an article about it on the computer in the library. A giant tunnelling machine is on its way from China to tunnel under the BP station. The tunnel will take three years to build. The same length of time it should take me to complete my degree.

I decided I had to see the road in the middle of the day in full sunlight. I walked for two hours from Albert Park back to the road in the heat of high noon. I sat on a wooden bench in the park next to the BP station and looked across at the construction site. I sat there and watched, as I imagined Mr Monet would have done when he painted the grain stacks, the cathedrals, the rivers in thaw – 'Les Glaçons'. And the light did change, as he showed it did. Clouds sauntered across the sky casting slow shade over the ground. The sun skimmed through the air on its own timetable. I sat and observed. The light changed and so did I. After two hours I walked back to the university and stood on the kerb waiting for my father to pick me up and take me home.

When he arrived, I opened the truck door and stood on the footpath staring into the cabin. I could see my father's red eyes framed in the rear vision mirror.

'What are you looking at? Get in!' he said.

My mother's shoulders stiffened at the sound of his voice. I climbed into the truck and wrenched the door shut. Racheli glanced at me with a questioning look and frowned.

From that day on, instead of going to lectures, I walked back to the road and sat on the wooden bench, enveloped in the ever-changing light covering the construction site and covering me. I sat on the bench for hours in rain, in morning light, in midday light. I watched the same scene, but it changed as I watched and learned. I had taken my education into my own hands, and I began to sense something would have to give.

On the morning it cracked open, we stood in the driveway waiting for my father to reverse out of the carport. I stood next to my mother, and saw a fresh purple bruise developing under her left eye. I hadn't seen a bruise on her face for a long time. I thought it had ended. She'd tried to tie her hair into a neat coil, as usual. But some fly wisps had dropped out of place and hung free around her jaw.

'This has to stop,' I said.

She started weeping. My father reversed the truck, and I could see him through the windscreen.

I shouted at him, pointing at my mother's face. 'You can't keep doing this!'

He jumped out of the truck and marched towards me. I stood shaking in front of my mother and my sister. He slapped me full across the face.

'Get in the truck!'

My head burned with pain. I refused to cry.

'No, I won't. You can't do this any more.'

His eyes blazed at me, his mouth curled over, and I saw his balled fist coming towards me. I jumped to one side and he stumbled, missing me by a centimetre. I saw my mother pick up his favourite silver socket wrench. She came up behind him and whacked him on the back with the wrench and he fell to the ground. She let go of the wrench and it dropped at her feet with a metallic thud. We stood for a moment in shock, fearful. Then I kicked him. I kicked with my whole weight as he lay on the driveway. I kicked him in the head, and in the guts, and in the head again. I kicked him hard, over and over until my legs hurt. My mother dragged on my arm but I shook myself free, stamping on him with my boot heel, as you would stamp on the top of a tin can to squash it flat. He groaned and tried to get up, but I kicked him in the head and he lay there in the gravel moaning, his face turning several shades of blood red and then black red and then grey. I stood puffing, gulping air, arms at the ready. My mother held her hands up to her face, looking at me, unbelieving. Racheli had retreated into the carport and stood cowering in the corner. I ran.

The construction site sounded busy. Trucks and cranes and bulldozers were throwing dust into the air. The sun channelled into a blazing slash of golden light tearing at the clouds. It was the same alien light I had seen before on the concrete barriers, the brilliant light I had longed to see again, shining for me once more: a gift, hovering in the sky, forcing its way through grey softness. One moment of molten light. I wanted to hold onto it. I knew it would end. I sat on the bench, transfixed, as the sun became a ball of pale orange surrounded by grey and white, filtered, ephemeral, and changing and beginning and ending. The changing light calmed me and stopped my racing thoughts, stayed my blood. I sat on the bench

Grain Stacks

for hours, until the light smoothed out. It turned pink before my eyes as the earth shifted on its axis. A warm rhythm played across my face, lulling me into a drowsy state, and I lay my head on the bench. I woke up in the dark. By 'dark', I mean the sun had gone. But there were huge lamps mounted high up on poles, lighting the entire scene. I had never seen the construction site at night. A security guard patrolled the fence line. The parked cranes sat quiet, swaying like trees in a forest.

I crept past the guard into the site and made my way into the cab of the blue crane. The inside of the cab smelled of rusty metal and diesel and sweat. But it was dry, and I fell asleep watching the stars over the construction site. The men and their machines did not cease at all, moving earth and hauling timber posts and lifting metal frames throughout the night. I dozed off then woke up and listened to the machinery humming, then dozed off again. I woke early the next morning to the sound of birds. The construction site was silent. I felt the cold morning air creeping into the crane and watched the rising sky turning milky orange.

I lay there staring at the view as the sun crept through the rigging of the yellow crane. Dragging my finger through a dirty oil patch on the gear housing, I traced a jagged ice floe circle, and then a grain stack triangle. My favourites are the golden summer grain stacks: forlorn, haunting, with their pointy grain heads catching the light like the yellow crane in the sunshine, or the glowing empty houses, or the lustrous thatched roofs of Fijian bures, sitting unencumbered on the ground, not flowing away like ice floes from a cracked river ice sheet. They sat still for one moment and Mr Monet saw them. Warm beacons of golden light.

Home Detention

At thirty-two years of age, Lucas did not want to go to jail. Not again. Jail and zoo, same thing. A carnival of human animals caged together every night and then let loose into the yard the next day. Let loose to wander about and look at the sky, and then turn on each other and then look at the sky and then hit out. This is where the bus ride began, outside the wooden door of the courthouse. He sat opposite the courtroom waiting for his name to sound through the intercom. He felt like a naughty kid waiting for school roll call, or an unemployed beneficiary waiting in line for a payment, or a sickness beneficiary waiting to see the doctor at the superclinic. This day would mark the first roll call of many if his luck didn't hold. Each of the seats in the waiting area held one, sometimes two or three people. As soon as someone vacated a seat, someone else would sit there, the tattered upholstery on view for a moment, picked away by many anxious fingers pulling loose threads, and then concealed again as people sat down in various states of apprehension and disarray. Silence would descend in the waiting area and you could hear movements and see heads turning and nodding and eyes large with fear.

A booming voice called a name over the loudspeaker system, the sound ringing and squealing in the subdued atmosphere. Everybody scanned the corridor to see who would answer to the name. A faint jostling and murmuring erupted in one corner. A man in black jeans and a black leather waistcoat over a black T-shirt shifted in his seat and turned his head as the name echoed in the hall. The woman seated next to him looked worried, and shrank behind his body. He twisted in his seat and whispered to her. Mollified, she gripped onto a washed-out green cloth bag as he led her in a slow drag past Lucas and up to the tall wooden door leading into the courtroom. The door opened to reveal a young woman in a severe black suit. She stood in sentry mode, waiting for the bewildered couple to enter.

The world behind the tall door revealed itself for an instant: a slice of ceiling-to-floor window shaded by ceiling-to-floor venetian blinds, the aluminium blades angled at 180 degrees, showing a view of the tree-lined river. Then the door swung shut. Lucas studied the wooden door: two wood veneer sheets cut lengthwise from a log of blonde wood rolled in a huge lathe and glued next to each other onto another piece of wood. The geometry created a mesmerising effect of opposing and identical cross grains meeting in the middle, a wooden kaleidoscope. The patterns reminded him of his six-year-old son Jacob's Spiderman kaleidoscope. Jacob would hold it up to one eye and clamp the other eye shut as he turned the tube with his tiny fingers, and squeal with joy as the pieces clicked in the tube.

Lucas's eyesight clouded with tears at the thought of Jacob. He hadn't seen his son for so long now. Not since the day CYFS had taken him away. Lucas clamped both eyes shut trying to drive the tears back inside his head. He squinted and blinked and concentrated on the door, looking for patterns in the wood until he saw a pair of large, upside down trousers. He folded his arms and sank back into his seat, trying to think about trousers and being upside down and not about Jacob. He didn't want to be blubbing in front of the court. He stretched his long legs out on the floor beside a band of liberated sunlight falling through the vertical window next to him. Closing his eyes to it, he had drifted off to sleep when the intercom squeaked into life and he heard the registrar call his name in a loud monotone: 'Lucas Buchanan.'

His turn. He walked to the tall door and when it opened for him, there stood the young woman in her dark Stasi suit. The courtroom felt stuffy, warm. People lolled about in the public gallery in bored states of bad posture. The lawyers sat with hunched backs poring over their papers. One of them turned in his seat and looked at Lucas. His lawyer, Mike Broz: young, serious, meticulous. The young woman in the black suit motioned Lucas to the witness box with a flat open-handed movement, as if she was performing semaphore on an airstrip or something. Lucas watched a bank of tired eyes in the public gallery, rolling in their sockets to see him walk from the door and into the dock. As he stood in the wooden box his mobile phone began to ring and vibrate in his jeans pocket. The judge looked over the bridge of her glasses at Lucas. He fumbled to retrieve the phone, but couldn't stop it ringing.

'Turn that phone off,' said the judge. She glared at Lucas from behind a large desk mounted several feet above the floor. A black gown cloaked her frame and flared onto the bench, making her look like a giant moth at rest. The phone would not stop trilling, ever louder and more insistent, the sound resonating in the cavernous room. Panicked, Lucas jabbed at the buttons. He turned the rubber-encased contraption around and over and pulled at the protective cover, trying to remove it so he could take out the battery. His fingers felt thick, as if he wore oven gloves. People in the gallery began to sit up straight, now interested, and amused. The lawyers uncurled their backs, abandoning their arguments with relief to watch the entertainment.

The tall door opened at the back of the courtroom. An unsuspecting man in a white shirt scuttled in and tried to find a seat in the public gallery. Taking a chance, Lucas lobbed the phone in the direction of the open door. A communal intake of breath rose audibly from the public gallery. The man in the white shirt froze, uncertain. Lucas pictured Jacob throwing an inflatable beach ball to him, its bright plastic panels tumbling in the air in slow motion and Jacob gleeful, bouncing in time with the ball as it touched on light brown sand.

The phone sailed in a high arc into the courtroom stratosphere, end over end, out of control, and disappeared through the tall door, which swept behind it in a soft hydraulic damper hush. Raucous laughter burst out from the public gallery. The lawyers' stifled mirth showed in their jiggling shoulders. Lucas looked with horror at the judge. She held her mouth firm, waiting for the disturbance in her courtroom to subside. Lucas felt unclear about whether she was trying to repress anger or amusement. Something threatened to spill out of her. The corners of her mouth may have curled upward. He couldn't tell.

'Yes, Sergeant Williams,' she said, straight-faced.

The laughter in the public gallery subsided at the sound of her imperious voice. A police prosecutor stood up in his blue uniform and sergeant stripes and read the charge sheets.

'Two charges, Your Honour. One charge possession precursors to manufacture methamphetamine. One charge possession equipment for use in manufacture of methamphetamine.'

Lucas's heart sank as he listened to the cop talk. He wanted to throw Lucas in the Big House, Rock College, Beirut Apartments.

He droned on and on about Lucas's prior convictions and the seriousness of the charges and how he should be locked up for years and left to rot in a hellhole of a jail with the rest of the animals. Then he sat in his chair puffed up and full of himself. The judge looked impenetrable, a gigantic black iceberg. But icebergs can melt, no matter how big they are. Isn't that why those islands somewhere in the wop wops are flooding? Because of the melting icebergs, he thought.

'Yes Mr Broz,' she said, her voice thinner this time.

Mike took centre stage, with his booming voice and dark royal Croatian bearing. Lucas's heart thumped so loud in his head, he heard Mike's words as single entities, curious carriages in a long train heading toward an unknown destination. Clinical – depression – hard – times – wrong – crowd – son – foster – care – steady – job – council– road – maintenance – pet – owner. Choo choo. The judge nodded, looked up from her papers and glanced at Lucas, who held her gaze for a second before looking away to the gallery. He felt glad his workmates hadn't turned up here to see him in this predicament. Working in the road gangs provided him with a sense of family: the luminescent variety, the hi-vis-orange-fluoro-vest-with-bright-yellow-piping-and-iridescent-silver-stripes-running-along-the-back-and-front variety. Operating the stop/go sign, feeding out orange cones in crooked rows from the back of the truck, sitting at smoko and puffing on cigarettes, and having a laugh with the rest of the road gang felt like the closest thing to family life he had at the moment, apart from his intermittent phone calls with Jacob. His boss Henare had written a letter to the judge. She took her time reading the letter silently, turning the courtroom into a silent cavern, holding the air enthralled and keeping Lucas in agony. The act of reading became a fulcrum, his freedom hanging in the balance. She had the power to take it away and throw him in the slammer, and she had the power to let him go. She shuffled her papers and sighed and looked at Lucas, and handed down a sentence of home detention, six months. It must have been a good letter. Thank you, Henare. The judge ordered Lucas to report to the police station once a week. She looked at him, stern, unmoving.

'I'm giving you one last chance.'

'Yes, Your Honour.'

'Any breaches and you will be sent straight to jail to serve out the remainder of your sentence. Do you understand, Mr Buchanan?'

'Yes, Your Honour.'

'Good. I don't want to see you here again.'

'Yes, sir. I mean, Your Honour.'

Lucas's ankle itched under the electronic bracelet. He bent over in his seat and burrowed his fingers beneath the rigid black plastic band around his lower tibia. Blood rushed into his head as he leaned forward into the silence of the afternoon. Today he must report. He must go to the police station and check in. He would not fail to report, no sir. No breach of home detention for him. No jail time, no thank you. The judge – he tried to remember her name, Scary Judge. He would not appear in front of her again. She would send him down. Blood pulsed in his ears, re-pressurising with the inverted position of his head; it became the new normal.

If he had succeeded in reaching gang headquarters with the Chinese pills and the glass beakers, he would have handed over the bags and left. Now he sat here stuck at home in compulsory softness, but still a prison, freedom beckoning over the fence line. Still, Scary Judge had saved his life, literally, and she would never know it. She would not know he would have been killed inside.

She allowed him to work on the roads with Henare. But he had to be home before curfew or the bracelet would sound an alarm somewhere in the bowels of Chubb Security and he would be picked up for breaching home detention and sent 'straight to jail'.

He never wanted to go to jail again; not now, not with the head of the Killer Beez inside. He would be toast. Not that he was a member of the Killer Beez. He was just a runner. The police caught him on his last run ever. Before the run, he'd decided to leave the criminal scene and go straight, and get his son back from foster care. Bad luck for him the police picked him up that day. But the Killer Beez wouldn't see it that way. Those guys were crazy. The drones would be sent out to deal with him. He would be dead meat. Thank you, Scary Judge.

Lucas had become the quintessence of punctuality. As he stood holding the stop/go sign at the roadworks, he would consult his watch, a black plastic brand from the supermarket: a matching set with his electronic leg bracelet. As he waited on the footpath for Henare to pick him up in the mornings, he would confer with the watch. As he stood at the bus stop in the evenings waiting for the bus to deliver him back to his one-bedroom home he would fold his arms and have a discussion with his watch.

'The 5.30 is running a bit late today.'

Once he stepped in the door, he relaxed. He would take off his watch – but the matching leg band would have to wait for another chafing six months. Such a long time, cooped up at night in a weatherboard state house. His neighbour Arnie Midgaard, seventy-three years old, wiry and red-faced with bushy white hair, had taken pity on him and given him some red cabbage and silverbeet to grow. Together that weekend, they dug up the short strip of lawn in front of Lucas's home and planted the seedlings in two rows. Lucas had never thought about gardening before. Tending the plants, side by side, now consumed his spare time: hand-picking bugs from their leaves, weeding and watering. He had grown one row of four red cabbages with large chalk-green leaves devolving into heads of red solid mass, and another row of flapping unruly silverbeet. Good going so far: two short rows of plants. But they had grown huge, and he enjoyed looking after them. Arnie praised his work in the garden.

Lucas had a dog waiting for him to get home after work every day, a skinny black and white Jack Russell. Jacob had named the creature 'Doglet' before the state took him away. A silly name for a dog. Now the dog kept Lucas company, and proved a lively topic of discussion with his son. The foster caregiver in Auckland would ring Lucas so that he could talk to Jacob, usually when his son had something momentous to talk about, such as getting a gold star from his teacher or tying his own shoelaces. But the dog was the main topic of discussion: did he have enough food? did he go for a walk? Did he chase the ball? Once they had exhausted talk about the dog, Jacob would hang up, too tired to talk any more. The discussion usually took maybe five minutes in total. Lucas loved to hear his son's voice. He longed to see him in person, to hug him and have a laugh with the little guy.

The leg still itched. From his doubled-over position he saw that the watch read 12.51 p.m. Lucas felt a slight rocking sensation as the earth moved underneath him. Nothing new. The white porcelain vase shook on top of the fridge. The vase belonged to his ex, Jacob's mum. She had left it on the fridge when she'd left him and Jacob and run off to Australia with some other bloke, and it stayed there on top of the fridge, threatening to fall in every aftershock since the big one had hit five months ago. The stupid vase could smash for all he cared: he had willed it to fall and shatter many times. But it had survived.

Today was Lucas's thirty-third birthday, and Henare had given him the day off. No such luck with the cops. He still had to report, birthday or not. He checked in with the watch.

'We need to catch the 1.30. Should take twenty-five minutes at this time of day.'

The skin under the ankle bracelet felt chafed and sore, but he kept scratching. He heard a low rumble, and a vibration moved through the seat of his chair. Then the whole room began to shake, and the vase took flight, hurtling through the air where his head would have been if he had been sitting upright. Lucky. He was never lucky. He heard the vase smash against the wall. The dog ran barking into the room.

'Doglet!'

The dog jumped into his lap, and he held him close. He tried to get out of the chair but the rocking floor pushed him down. Sash windows rattled. The rumble should have stopped after a few minutes, but it kept going. What crockery he had in the cupboards clinked together and slid through the cupboard doors, cascading in a china waterfall and crashing onto the bench below. The table moved in front of him. His cup of tea fell onto the floor together with a carton of milk and a pink packet of sugar. A tea puddle slopped white and brown back and forth across the lino. The moving floor threw him off his chair, and the dog went flying. Lucas crawled under the table as it danced on the floor. His heart thumped in his chest. The dog ran back to him, yelping. Kauri floorboards bucked and undulated in waves under the lino, tossing him about, but he managed to keep hold of the dog. This is it, he thought. I'm done for.

Two windows along the back wall curved inwards until the glass exploded and sprayed Lucas and the dog. He curled himself over the dog to protect him. Doglet barked and whimpered in equal measure. The house pitched and rolled and threw them across the floor. Lucas's dark hair fell about his face in time with the rocking house. Car alarms and house alarms wailed in the street outside. He slid back across the floor and huddled under the table with the dog. He hoped the shaking would stop, soon. The noise was like a freight train in the hallway, an unearthly sound. The bucking subsided into slow trembling as the earth settled like an animal circling to find a comfortable place to lie down, twitching and shuddering until calm silence descended.

The contents of the cupboards and drawers had disgorged into the room and somehow sculpted themselves into drifts of debris. A rainbow of food had fallen out of the fridge. A smashed bottle oozed red tomato sauce, egg yolks dripped in thick golden tears and a bruised red cabbage lay dejected among broken crockery. A large jagged gap at the top of one wall opened out into the sky, and the corner of the ceiling hung in tatters. Glass shards sparkled in the sunlight shining through a brand new hole in the ceiling. A snapped floorboard stuck through the lino. The floor now bent into a lean. Lucas's breath rasped in and out of his throat as he watched a potato roll from the high end of the room to join a growing pile of rubble in the opposite corner. The dog shivered and whimpered in his arms. Lucas cast his eyes upward, waiting, choking in the swirling dust.

A warm trickle of blood ran along his arm into the dog's face. He tried to find cuts on the dog, and then saw a piece of glass sticking out of his own forearm. A surface wound, but the blood flow would not stop. He put the dog onto the crooked floor, his white fur face a pink shade of human blood. He picked out the glass shard from his flesh and tore a strip from the bottom of his shirt, then wrapped it tightly around the gash.

Crawling over the rubble, scraping his knees as he went, he made his way through the house. The whole structure leaned and creaked. A frozen chicken lay in the hallway. His old red couch protruded from the lounge door, blocking entry. His bedroom door wouldn't budge. The familiar iridescent silver stripes of his hi-vis vest peeked out from under an upended bookcase. Lucas yanked at the vest to extract it, and then put it on over his ripped shirt. The front door had been pried from its hinges, and lay broken and splintered on the deck. By some miracle the garden had stayed intact, the prized red cabbages and silverbeet safe in their beds. The air felt cool and still and unaware. Silent pine trees lined the street, ominous against a blue sky. The usual weka call was absent. A distant background roar from the ocean had always comforted Lucas. Now it held a menacing echo of earthquake.

The dog stuck close to his side, barking, as Lucas hobbled along the street. The world was a disaster movie. A blue geyser gushed from a burst water main in the middle of the street. The asphalt road surface had disintegrated into a frothing watercourse channelling silt and sewerage downhill. The bus wouldn't be able to drive on the road with so much gunk covering it, he thought. He would have to walk to the cop shop.

People lay dazed in the road or ran or walked like zombies from *Dawn of the Dead*. The ground continued to rumble, and people shrieked and hugged each other, looking about in terror. Lucas heard a chainsaw buzzing next door at Arnie's. As he walked around the corner he could see the old man sawing a hole in the side of his house, his bushy white hair sprouting beneath a bicycle helmet perched on top of his head. He turned off the machine as Lucas approached.

'You all right, Arnie?'

'Yeah, I'm fine. Biggest shake I've felt for a while. The house shifted on its foundations. She'll fall any minute.'

'What are you doing?'

'Getting the work out. Can you help me?'

Arnie was a famous artist. Lucas had seen stories about him in the papers. One of Arnie's paintings had sold for seventy-five thousand dollars. Imagine it. So much dough for splashing a bit of paint on a canvas. Lucas did like the shapes, though, and the colours made him think of summertime in Auckland at the beach with Jacob.

'I gotta report.'

'They won't care about that today.'

'Yeah they will. They'll send me to jail if I don't check in.'

Arnie sat on the ground and began to cry. Oh no, not the waterworks. He always does this. Lucas saw him on TV once when he won some award. The old duffer bawled then too. And after the last quake he had blubbered as well.

The dog nudged Arnie's leg.

'I've worked on these pieces for months,' he said, patting the dog.

'If it means so much to you, I'll give you a hand. But then I have to go,' said Lucas.

Arnie's face lit up. He got to his feet and restarted the chainsaw. Lucas blocked his ears until Arnie completed cutting out a circle of weatherboard from the side of his house. The splintered disc of wood fell into the house with a clatter. A dusty, swirling interior revealed itself upon a ray of sunlight. Arnie climbed into the hole. Lucas followed as closely as possible behind the old weirdo. Wooden-framed paintings, sheets of canvas and paint tins littered the room. Arnie picked up the side of a stretched canvas, splashed with dusty blobs of red and streaks of black, orange and white in no order. Lucas helped carry the strange picture through the hole in the wall, feeling like a Beagle Boy.

'What's this one called?' he asked.

'"Rūaumoko Turns". He's the god of earthquakes,' said Arnie.

Bloody stupid thing to paint as far as Lucas was concerned. Tempting fate. They had to make several trips to get the paintings out of the wrecked house and into the old man's shed: a metal box, built in the corner of the yard. Although the February afternoon blew hot, Lucas felt cold under his ripped and bloodstained hi-vis. While Arnie tended his precious artworks, Lucas zipped the dog into the hi-vis and helped himself to Arnie's mountain bike, cycling away without a word. The old codger worried too much about his grimy old paintings; they meant nothing to Lucas.

An inexorable force propelled Lucas towards the police station: that force being the need to eliminate the risk of spending any time incarcerated in a tiny prison cell constructed out of concrete blocks during a time of high earthquake activity. His diligent reporting would show compliance with the sentence Scary Judge had pronounced and, he hoped, earn him early parole, again keeping him out of the dreaded prison cell and safe from cave-ins; not to mention murder at the hands of drug-addled gangsters.

As he cycled around the corner into Market Street, Lucas heard a woman call for help. He stopped the bike. Doglet barked and kicked, struggled out of the hi-vis and jumped onto the road. Lucas watched the dog as he picked a path into a ruined house towards a woman who was lying in full view of the street. The whole side of her house was destroyed. She lay pinned under a toppled shower cubicle: an elderly woman with blue eyes and a wounded head, blood dripping down the side of her face and into her long grey hair. Oh God, she had no clothes on. What a bloody nuisance. He swung himself off the bike and walked over the piles of ruined wood into her shattered home. Using a broken strut, Lucas levered the shower cubicle off the old woman. She looked pale and drawn, and she was shivering as he wrapped her in bath towels he'd found scattered about in the bathroom rubble.

'Nothing broken?' he asked.

She didn't reply, and sat gazing at the devastated bathroom. Blood flowed from a gash in her head. A surface wound, like his own.

'She'll be right. A surface cut,' he said, dabbing her head gently with a towel. 'What's your name?'

'Moira.'

Lucas put his hands on Moira's shoulders and guided her over to Arnie's shed. The dog trotted alongside them, yapping. Arnie emerged from the hole in the wall as they arrived.

'Arnie, this is Moira. I found her holding an open home down the road,' said Lucas.

He expected a laugh from both of them. But the woman stared at him, unblinking, and Arnie disappeared on another spelunking expedition into the house, emerging minutes later with a red and black plaid shirt and a pair of blue overalls.

'Not the best. But they should fit you,' he said, handing the clothes to the woman.

Lucas settled Moira on a tarp in the sunshine with Doglet, who sat leaning into her back.

Arnie's clothing rested in a pile in her lap, and she pulled the bath towels tight around her shoulders.

'Can you look after the dog while I go to report?' said Lucas.

'Okay, son. But surely they won't make you report today,' said Arnie.

'I have to or the judge will send me to jail.'

'Can you take this and fill it up before you leave?' said Arnie, handing Lucas a large plastic water container.

Lucas looked at his watch and grabbed the container. He took it to mollify the old man and tied it to the handlebars of the bike. He rode into the warm black smoky day with no intention of fetching any water.

As he cycled along Market Street he saw a large hole in the side of a house where a boulder had fallen down the hill, smashed through flimsy wood and rolled out the other side. Light reflected from inside the house and into Lucas's face as he rode past. He stopped the bike to take a look and saw smashed glass and rifles scattered around the base of an old gun cabinet. A silver pistol glinted in the rubble. He thought about taking the gun, as it might come in handy if he came across the Killer Beez buzzing around, but he quickly rethought, and left it alone. The odds of the police finding a stolen pistol on him when he reported were higher that those of bumping into any of the Killer Beez.

He continued riding along Market Street. Dust blew out of his hair and trailed in a dark slipstream behind him. He didn't see the silver four-wheel-drive vehicle until it appeared in front of him. He hit the side, and rolled over the bonnet. The water container hit him in the face and bounced onto the road. He fell on the ground and immediately stood up. The vehicle screeched to a halt a few metres away.

'What the fuck are you doing?' he yelled.

The roof of the vehicle was staved in as if a slab of concrete had fallen on it. The windscreen was cracked but remained whole, in one curved and bumpy sheet. Written in large lettering on the side of the vehicle were the words 'Niuean Solar Panel & Installation Limited. Nukai Talagi, Director'. The driver was a man in a pinstriped suit. He glared at Lucas and climbed out of the driver's door.

'You wrecked my bike.'

'Ka ule!' shouted the man.

He left the engine running and ran to Lucas, muttering in a foreign language, probably Niuean. A woman emerged from the passenger side of the vehicle in a fitted red dress and black shoes and ran to join them.

'Are you alright?' said the man.

'I have to get to the police station.'

The couple looked at each other. Lucas took his chance and sprinted over to their idling vehicle. He jumped in, heaved the crumpled door shut and drove away, with his foot to the floor and the tyres squealing. The steering pulled severely to the left. He struggled to keep the truck in the middle of the street. He saw the couple as he veered around a corner. The man ran towards him, and the woman stood still, resigned, watching him. As he turned the corner at the end of Market Street an old brick tower toppled into the road in front of the truck. He slammed on the brakes and jammed the gear stick into reverse as an aftershock buckled and curled the road. Another building crashed to the ground behind him, trapping him, surrounding him with piles of brick and collapsed buildings. He left the truck and clambered over the rubble in the direction of where he thought he would find the police station. He needed some time to reorient himself to the new landscape. The familiar markers, buildings, street names: everything destroyed. He climbed over wrecked cars and buildings. The Niuean man, where was he?

A removal truck lay on its side, blocking his way. A house-lot of furniture had tumbled out of the truck into a heap. Lucas squeezed between the now vertical roof of the truck and a large sideboard. Layers of books had spilled from cardboard boxes. He found them slippery to walk over. He put his right foot on *The New Zealand Wars*, and it slid like a skateboard until he stamped his left foot on *Crime and Punishment*, which moved and pitched him to his hands and knees, carrying him along in an avalanche of books until his forehead rested on *End as a Man* by Calder Willingham. He'd always taken notice of the titles of books. He just never understood the inside. Damn books! At least with bricks and cars he could gain some purchase, more solid footing. Hundreds of books in a heap turned into a moving liquid surface, and he struggled to be free of them and get back onto his feet. But then more books fell, like paper water, submerging him. With a mammoth wrench, Lucas heaved himself up and surfaced, gulping for air and shaking himself off like Scrooge McDuck swimming in money: his kind of reading.

He sprinted away from the books and did not stop until he rounded a familiar corner to find the police station had changed into a smoking jumble of girders and masonry. A storm of shredded paper filled the air, flaring and turning black on contact with sparking wires. There were police officers running around the ruined building, stamping out flames with their boots.

A young police officer tapped Lucas on the shoulder.

'Hey buddy, can you give us a hand here? We need more of you guys to get people out of the cells,' she said, pointing to the side of the stricken building.

Lucas saw people wearing hi-vis vests the same as he wore: rescue workers, firefighters, police officers and ordinary people, throwing aside rubble. He ran to help. Trapped below the surface in a holding cell he saw several police officers and prisoners shouting directions, their faces powdered white with dust as rescuers hauled them up with thick red plastic ropes. The rescuers hauled up eight people one by one. Lucas stood at the front of the rope line, holding the winch steady and peering into the hole alongside several firefighters in yellow coats. As he stood watching the last police officer being winched up, an aftershock struck. Dangling on the end of the rope, the police officer swung back and forth. Lucas lost balance and fell into the hole, into darkness, onto a concrete floor, a dull thud ... thud ... thud repeating next to him as he blacked out.

'Dad, Dad, where's Doglet?'
   'Jacob?'
   'Where is he, Dad? He has to have a bath.'

'What are you doing here? How'd you get …'

'Where's his shampoo? Y'know, the one that smells like strawberries?'

'Jacob, listen to me, son. Leave now. You're not safe here.'

'Oh, here it is, Dad – you put it in the food cupboard, silly!'

Lucas felt the itch of the bracelet on his ankle and reached down his leg to scratch the irritated skin. A searing pain shot into his calf. He tried to scream, but no noise came out. His head throbbed. He didn't feel right. He couldn't see, and he felt cold and suffocated. He coughed. Not dead. Someone touched his face.

'You're okay.'

'Hello?'

'You'll be all right.'

'I'm blind,' said Lucas.

'No you're not.'

A blue light flared in the darkness.

'Where am I?' said Lucas.

'In a hole, mate. We're in a hole.'

The blue light retreated, a mobile phone light, and then it snuffed out, leaving a sunburst orange impression on the back of Lucas's eyelids.

'How long?' said Lucas.

'Been here 'bout twelve hours now.'

Tapping noises echoed somewhere. Lucas lifted himself into a seated position. His head swam. He couldn't breathe, and his ankle burned like fire. The voice breathed heavily next to him. Lucas reached his arm towards the sound, then pulled back.

'I'm Lucas.'

'David.'

'I don't feel so good.'

'Your leg is broken. I tried to stabilise it.'

Lucas touched the ragged material wrapped around his ankle. The tapping noises grew louder, and the air above them crumbled until a bright light shone through a hole. A disembodied hand reached in and waved, followed by a face wearing a firefighter's helmet.

'Hello. We're gonna get you out. Is anyone hurt?' said the firefighter.

David yelled something, but Lucas couldn't make it out. He could see David's face and his mouth moving and his blue police shirt with sergeant stripes on the sleeves. Lucas looked at the end of his leg. His foot lay at a strange angle, and didn't look like it was a part of him. Waves of pain coursed through his body. A drilling noise started above their heads and then stopped. They sat in silence for a long time.

'I'm on home D. I came in to report,' said Lucas.

'In the middle of an earthquake?'

'Yeah,' said Lucas, falling silent and feeling foolish.

'Today's my birthday,' he said.

'Happy birthday.'

'I have a son called Jacob. He's six.'

Lucas reached for his wallet and removed a photograph of Jacob and Doglet that he kept with him at all times. But he couldn't see it clearly in the dark.

'Here,' said David, shining a torch light from his phone onto the photo in Lucas's hand.

'My son Jacob. I bought the dog for him.'

'He's a fine lad. My son Harry is studying science at university. I have pictures of him,' said David, shifting his body to one side.

He took out his wallet and retrieved two tattered photos with feathery edges and shone his phone torch on them for Lucas to see. Lucas looked at a picture of David next to a smiling young man with curly black hair, sitting on a rock above a lake.

'Waikaremoana last summer. Me, the wife and Harry and our daughter Gemma. And this is one of me and Harry when he was a toddler.'

'I didn't know my dad,' said Lucas.

He started coughing and passed out. When he woke he could see a steel rope lowering into the hole with a basket chair attached to it. The chair swung back and forth suspended above the floor.

A firefighter yelled from above, 'Get in and clip the safety. Hurry, there's not much time.'

Lucas held on as David lifted him into the chair. He screamed in pain as the broken bones in his ankle ground together. David clipped the safety harness across Lucas's chest, climbed onto the back bar of the chair and held onto the rope. A winch motor started, and the chair began rising into the air. Lucas held onto the metal webbing and looked at the hole above him as the chair jerked upwards. But it stopped halfway, swaying from side to side in the air.

'What's wrong?' said Lucas.

He heard shouting above and a rumbling noise, as an aftershock vibrated through the earth and the chair jerked and hopped in the air.

'Hang on,' said David.

The firefighters hauled on the steel rope, pulling the chair up manually, hand over hand. The ground rumbled again, and chunks of debris hit David. He lost his grip on the chair and fell to the floor. The firefighters held on above as David scrambled onto the back bar of the chair, but his added weight made it too difficult for the firefighters to pull the chair up again. David let go. As he fell to the floor, the chair jerked upwards, and Lucas screamed in pain. The ground roared in the confined space as the chair hoisted up, up and up through the roof and out to safety. The ground shook again, and the roof caved into the hole.

As Lucas lay in the ambulance he reached down to scratch under the electronic bracelet, his ankle itching as it always did. He felt something feathery tucked in there, and pulled the object out. He unfolded a crumpled photo. As he stared at it through a haze of pain he thought the boy in the photo looked like Jacob. But he realised that it was David's son, Harry, and that the man in the photo was a younger version of David.

Glacier

Stig Andersson talked to a supervisor at the cut-to-length line on the factory floor as two female police officers arrived from Polismyndigheten i Stockholms län. He showed them to his office, where one of the police officers stood with heavy eyes and said that they had great regret in telling him that his wife Greta had had an accident; she had fallen onto the train tracks at Stockholm Central Station, and she had died at the scene.

Stig was therefore shocked when he received an email from Greta two days after her death. Owing to the unfathomable vagaries of the internet, her email had lingered in the ether for two days, until it bobbed into the light like a dormant mine. The subject line read 'Happy anniversary älskling.' He hung his head with the realisation that he had forgotten their anniversary. There was no message with the email, just an attachment containing two return airline tickets and an itinerary for a guided hiking tour in New Zealand. She had killed herself on their anniversary day. But if had she taken her own life, why were there two tickets? He blamed himself.

Their annual hiking expeditions had taken them to mountains and rivers and outlying pockets of the planet untouched by the light and the pollution of great conurbations of people toiling into the darkness. They hadn't visited New Zealand. The closest they had come was when they hiked the Larapinta Trail in Central Australia. Stig had rolled his ankle on the fifth day, and a rescue helicopter had had to airlift him to the start of the trail at Alice Springs. Greta had carried on to see the view from Mount Sonder, while Stig sat with his leg propped up in bed at Alice Springs Hospital next to an Arrernte man who had fallen from a grandstand at the Camel Cup race.

Now here he sat, without her, bereft, hiding in a hotel foyer in Auckland. The hotel was a converted 1950s department store, stripped back to the old concrete, with modern plate-glass walls. At nearby tables office workers were sitting down for breakfast meetings. He observed a man with enormous calves wearing khaki shorts and tramping boots looking up, mesmerised, at the ice-crystal chandelier sparkling in the curved atrium above his head.

Calf-man had blonde hair, blue eyes, dishevelled clothes and a compact body. Stig watched as the hotel receptionist pointed the man in his direction. He took a newspaper from the glass coffee table and opened it out wide like a sail in front of his face, pretending to read.

'Hello, I'm Norman Whitehouse,' the man said, peering over the edge of the newspaper.

Stig crumpled the daily into his lap, trying to fold it into a messy flat square as he peeled his body away from the comfort of the chair and stood up tall and lithe. Norman's eyes opened wide as if he had a glandular problem. The whites of his eyeballs framed his irises.

He looked insane. He tilted his head sideways and looked at Stig like a swivel-head puppy, his hand outstretched, hovering between them. Stig shook his hand.

'Yes, hello. My name is Stig Andersson.'

'Will your wife be joining us?'

'I'm sorry, my wife isn't here. It's just me.'

'Well ... that's a shame,' said Norman.

Stig could not speak. Greta should be here with him. When she killed herself she knew she was sending him alone to the other side of the earth. Of course, he needn't have taken her up on it. He could have stayed in his office at the steel mill, poring over the paperwork. But he had no stomach for it; he needed to move. He tried to recall her face and had to concentrate hard for a moment. He saw her tramping along the leaf-strewn paths of the forests in Nordland, asleep in a bearskin in the ice palace, gazing at the Northern Lights flickering purple and green across the horizon, spellbound beneath a welter of stars in the Grand Canyon. He turned away to grab his pack.

'I have my bag here.'

'Well, I'm sure you'll enjoy the next few days,' said Norman.

Norman clutched the steering wheel and kept his mad eyes on the road ahead as he drove to Karamatura Valley. They moved at speed into the scruffy hinterland of the city and the rural lifestyle blocks and out towards the coast. Lush greenery crowded over their heads as they climbed from an isolated coastal settlement into a winding road skirting large kauri trees. In a one-sided conversation, Norman pointed out landmarks to Stig and told him Māori legends about the area as they drove deeper into the bush and the terrain rose up above them on all sides.

Stig shifted uneasily in his seat and watched the scenery flash past. As Norman turned the truck into a side road Stig saw two men assaulting each other on the verge. A woman stood somehow in between them. Was that Greta? Norman ignored them, and continued looking straight ahead through the front windscreen. Stig twisted in his seat-belted restraint to get a better look at the woman as they sped past. He watched her until she had receded far into the background, and then untwisted himself to look at Norman.

'Bit of silliness, those people,' Norman said.

The scenery became mountainous. Norman steered the truck into a dirt driveway and they entered a primeval world. Ancient trees soared overhead, their branches draped with tangled foliage blotting out the sunlight. Stig sighed with relief when they emerged into a clearing filled with parked cars. Chattering Japanese tourists disembarked from oversized late model BMWs and milled about in groups. They wore crisp fawn safari vests with lots of utilitarian pockets, and carried huge black cameras with long lenses. Norman stepped out of the truck and hauled a heavy pack from the back of the vehicle and onto his back. Stig shouldered a daypack for his clothing as Norman loaded his pack with supplies. He turned his attention to the Japanese tourists gathering in large family clusters of parents and children and grandparents: something he would never have. Something Greta never had. He took a flat silver flask from his hip pocket and sipped the hot vodka in an attempt to cauterise his biological failure. No heir to take over the mill after he died.

'A huge glacier carved out this valley in the Ice Age,' Norman said.

Stig studied the bare rock walls towering on each side of the valley. He felt empty in this place of sheer grey desolation and scrubby growth. His thoughts tapered into the narrow bands of his life, and he sensed a mild panic invade his careful and cultivated exterior.

'Lots of waterfalls in there. We'll be abseiling into some of them tomorrow,' Norman said, tightening the ties on his backpack.

A creeping dread overwhelmed Stig's senses, and he longed for the comfort of familiar routines, checking smelters and furnaces and hot rollers and slabs of metal. This 'being out in nature' gig felt pointless and empty without Greta. He imagined hanging in the cold flow of a waterfall and shuddered. Absurd. He resolved to resign himself to it.

The track started on gentle sloping grassland growing on the ancient banks of moraine. As they entered the valley the bush closed behind them. The track followed a high drop-off and fell away to a narrow stream of water.

'This is your walk, so I'll go at a pace you find comfortable.'

Wonderful, Stig thought, rolling his eyes to the valley walls far above the ground. He trudged in silence behind Norman in the manner of a condemned man following his executioner. Norman stopped along the path and held out a leaf as wide as his hand.

'This is rangiora. It's very strong. You can write on it, use it for toilet paper.'

Stig touched the white furry underside of the leaf. He understood how it could be used for toilet paper, but why would anyone want to write on a leaf? He picked one anyway and stuffed it into his jacket pocket.

'This is koromiko,' said Norman, standing next to a low spreading shrub.

Shiny green leaves grew from the stems at odd angles.

'Māori used to pick the leaf tips and send them to the troops in the Second World War. It cures dysentery.'

Stig recalled his grandfather's stories of being forced to supply steel to the Nazi war machine during World War II for making bombs and Messerschmitts. Now Stig owned the steel mill, and sold steel to the Germans for their high-spec cars.

'This is tutu. A highly poisonous plant. I once saw a horse eat half a branch and drop dead right in front of me.'

Norman pointed at the plant but did not touch it. 'Māori made wine with it. They filtered it through nīkau leaves. If even one berry got through, it would kill them. I suppose they had their slaves test it first.'

Norman's eyes shone with wonder – or was it amusement? There was no way of knowing how to respond to him. The berries looked like tiny spherical beads with a purply orange gloss. Stig found them unimpressive. He knew of many poisonous plants in the forest behind his house in Stockholm. He picked three smooth tutu berries and placed them in his jacket pocket along with the rangiora leaf and the koromiko tips. Maybe later, when he could hide alone in his tent, he would strain the tutu and some vodka through the rangiora leaf. Norman kept pointing out plants to him. Stig wondered if he was going to explain the entire living dispensary.

Ahead of him, Norman stripped an oval leaf from a sapling and instructed Stig to eat the white strip at the base of the stem.

'It tastes like carrot, doesn't it? But you'd have to strip the entire plant to get a decent feed.'

Further down the track, Norman cut a shoot off what he said was a supplejack creeper and peeled the tender bark away before handing it to Stig, indicating he should try it. It tasted like asparagus.

'These orange berries have caffeine in them. You can make a decent cup of coffee with them. Just don't mix them up with tutu. This plant is good for toothache. This one is good for indigestion ...'

Stig wondered whether he could brew a tutu coffee. Logic dictated that if Māori considered it safe to filter tutu for wine, he could also filter it for coffee with no ill effects. And if it didn't work, well ... he would be with Greta, wouldn't he? And they would be together again, free. He held on for another hour – half listening half dreaming, while Norman persisted in explaining the medicinal properties of native herbs and the names of snails and birds and trees. As the path widened Norman fell into step beside him. Stig realised Norman had stopped talking about the plants and had changed the topic to himself.

'An old tohunga taught me these things when I was young. He could move about in the bush like a ghost. He rang me one day and told me he didn't have long to go. They found him that afternoon sitting in a chair on his porch. He was ninety-nine years old. All the Māori people up north used say to me "How come you know this stuff? You're a Pākehā". He just picked me for some reason. I don't know why. I love the bush, so maybe he thought I should know about it.'

Like Stig cared. As he rounded a bend in the path, he stopped. Before him lay a large oblong boulder near an overhanging stone outcrop. Moisture seeped through bright green moss covering the stone and dripped with a musical echo into a pool of water. He stood and absorbed the light play in the pool as it shone against his face and settled into his retinas, calming him for the first time since the police officers had told him about the train incident.

'This is a beautiful spot.'

Norman explained that they were standing at the site of an ambush where seven people had been killed in a battle between the families of two warring brothers.

'I had to lift the tapu. There's a sentry over there on the rock. He looks after the place,' Norman said, pointing at the boulder next to Stig.

'He gets a bit annoyed at all the people passing him by every day. No one says hello to him.'

Stig walked closer to the boulder, which lay squat on the ground, flat on top and as high as his chest. He could see no one there.

'His name is Hānui. He told me to be careful with you. You've brought someone with you and she's not happy.'

'What are you talking about? I can't see anyone,' said Stig.

'I thought I saw a woman sitting near you at the hotel, and now she's sitting on the rock talking to Hānui.'

Stig walked away from the boulder and over to the pool of water, his hands on his hips. He gazed at Norman, shook his head and took a sip from his hip flask. Norman stood firm and held Stig's attention. Several other trampers appeared on the track and walked past them.

'I can see them,' said Stig sarcastically, pointing at the trampers' backs as they passed him. 'But I can't see your sentry or your woman.'

'Okay,' said Norman, staring at Stig. 'Let's go.' And he returned to the track.

This had happened in the Grand Canyon. A guide from the Havasupai Reservation had seen a young girl following Stig and Greta. But there was no one there. Stig reasoned it must be part of the deal on these trips. There had to be an obligatory ghost or ghoul sighting or some weird event to add to the atmosphere.

They climbed for five hours and arrived at the base of a tall waterfall. Mist wafted from a dark green pool at the foot of the rock face. The water flowed into a channel and over another precipitous drop into the next pool far below them, and on and on in a continuing giant staircase of waterfalls. Stig slumped onto his pack, thankful to stop for the day, while Norman set up the tents on a patch of grass. The sound of roaring water was strangely comforting. As night closed in Stig sat alone in his tent, sipping on the hip flask and watching insects dance on his torch light. He wrote Greta's name in blue pen on the papery rangiora leaf and put it into his pocket.

At 3.30 a.m. he woke in a haze. The rush of water filled his ears, reminding him of the sound of a train in a tunnel. He felt cold and cramped in the dark stuffy tent. After groping around and finding the torch he stumbled into the night, sweeping the light beam from side to side. He remembered tramping in the Dordogne with Greta. How he had wanted a happy life with her. How they'd tried to have children. Greta had taken special leave from her work at Stockholm University. She told him she wanted to rest, to get ready. He carried on running the steel mill.

He didn't want to live without her. He couldn't manage it. He had failed her. She'd taken the easy way out. They were supposed to grow old together. He walked towards the edge of the waterfall and shone the torch into the darkness below. Billowing puffs of vapour swallowed the beam of light. He imagined her standing on the railway platform, waiting for the train, timing it, stepping off. Did she think of him? Why did she do it? The thrashing sound of the water was relentless. The train was coming and she just jumped. How did she get to that point? She'd said nothing to him that morning. She looked happy. It would be so easy to just step off into the void. He lifted one foot and shifted his weight forward. He teetered on the rocky lip of the waterfall – and toppled over backwards as Norman's splayed hands grabbed him around the waist and pulled him away from the brink.

Norman was nowhere to be seen the following morning. Stig returned to the rocky edge at the top of the waterfall. Unlike the night before, the water now flowed smoothly and peacefully into the pool below. He saw Greta out of the corner of his eye and spun to welcome her. But it was just Norman emerging from the greenery.

'Are you all right this morning, mate?'

'My back is sore,' said Stig, stepping away from the edge.

He folded his arms to keep away the chill rising up from the water, and contemplated the emptiness of the valley.

'You know …' Norman's voice trailed off as the water hurried past them and carried on down the giant waterfall staircase on its way to the sea. '… Hānui said it was an accident.'

Stig looked up to the sky at the end of the giant corridor above them.

The police had told him the platform was crowded that day. Witnesses reported that she just fell without warning.

He stared in awe at the sheer rock walls on either face of the valley: towering, imposing, glazed with early morning mist. The glacier was long gone, but it had left a clear and breathtaking path, a ghostly U-shaped gap where ice had once pushed its way through rock and earth and left its indelible mark on the landscape forever. Way up high near a dark-veined rock intrusion on the north face, a beam of sunlight caught the gold brindle wingspan of a hawk floating into the stillness of the chasm. Stig watched the hawk's flight path until he could no longer see it against the mass of green foliage lining the valley walls and growing into the crevices. Unfolding his arms, he placed his hands into his pockets, and felt something spiky poke into his left hand. He pulled his hand away in surprise, reflexive, thinking he had been hurt. But he realised there was no pain. He smoothed the surface of the crumpled rangiora leaf inside his pocket and it flattened out soft and warm in his hand.

Black Ice

Passang touched his numb cheek as he left the dental surgery. He felt no connection with his own skin, as if his hand floated on the cold surface of someone else's flesh. Passang's name in Sherpa meant 'Friday'. He was born on Friday, same as his older brother, Passang, and his younger sister, also Passang.

A taxi swerved into the kerb next to him. A startling manoeuvre, but since the car was a taxi he was unsurprised. The passenger door flew open, and alcohol fumes wafted out from the dank interior of the vehicle. A drunk white man with dishevelled red hair and ratty teeth slurred and cursed at the driver, a man of indeterminate racial heritage, maybe North Indian, Western Turkish, Northern Chinese or Croatian. He sat impassive, his tweed cheese-cutter meeting the edge of black horn-rimmed glasses.

'You are a Muslim prick,' said the passenger.

'Why?' said the taxi driver.

'Because you come over here and ... why don't you just fuck off back to where you came from?'

'The camera is recording you.'

'Don't you threaten me, you prick!'

'I'm just saying there's a camera in here recording you.'

'You just blither out crap ... you Islam filth.'

'Okay.'

'Are you from New Zealand?'

'I told you. I'm not from here.'

'So you're here to infiltrate our country.'

The taxi driver's tone remained gentle, exasperated.

'Seven dollars. If you want to pay me now it's good. Okay?'

'Why can't you just fuck off and go back to where you came from?'

'I will go. But first pay me, okay?'

'I'll pay you seven bucks when you tell me that you'll piss off back to the country you came from. You shouldn't be in New Zealand in the first place. We don't require your Muslim bullshit.'

Passang saw the passenger pull a hunting knife from his jacket and wave it at the driver. The driver left the engine running and ran onto the footpath next to Passang. The drunk passenger fell out of the cab and onto his own knife, stabbing himself in the chest.

Passang forgot his anaesthetised face and rushed to the man, much as he'd reached out two days ago to the woman who'd tripped over her crampon ties and cartwheeled her arms trying to right herself on the ice. In mid-flight she'd spun her elbow into Passang's face and broken his front tooth clean in half. Passang fell to his knees next to the man and held his hands on each side of the knife to stop the bleeding. Deep red blood pulsed over his splayed fingers, spattering the gold letters on the knife handle: 'Helico Hydraulics'.

'What's your name?' Passang asked him.

'Malcolm Buttworth,' he said, and passed out.

Passang kept the pressure around the knife wound until the ambulance arrived.

The taxi driver was Bilal Dareshak from Pakistan. Bilal showed the police the camera footage of Mr Buttworth's abusive tirade in the taxi, followed by his fall onto the knife, followed by Passang saving his life.

'He should get a medal,' said Bilal, jabbing his finger at Passang.

The following morning Passang drove out of Queenstown on State Highway Six towards Fox Glacier Township. He slowed down on the dark road through the Kawarau Gorge. Traffic signs emblazoned with the words 'Black Ice' shone iridescent orange in the car's headlights. Passang knew to concentrate on the road ahead and not get distracted by the turquoise river glowing in the gorge below. This stretch of road had seen many vehicles slide out of control, smash through the barriers and plummet over the bank into the icy water. He peered at the road for any glossy sheen of black ice. Approaching the end of the gorge, he spotted a change in the asphalt. The tar smoothed out, and tiny shadows disappeared. He felt the car pull into a spin, and turned the wheels into the skid. The car fishtailed and slid back on course.

As he drove into Fox Glacier Township, shadowy mountains rose above him. He steered the car straight to the office of Blue Glacier Tours.

'Hey Daddy Sherpa, you're famous! Good to have you back. We've got a full book today,' said Bernard Galway.

Passang was always respectful of the owner's youngest son.

'Not such a great day for it, Bernard.'

Outside the rain had started to fall, and clouds had settled over the summits of Mount Tasman and Mount Cook. The guides in the boot room busied themselves preparing for the first group of the day. Andrea was at the counter putting the sock bins out. As Passang bounced into the room, she straightened her lean, tall frame and tossed her brown hair to one side with a laugh.

'Hey hero Sherpa. We saw you on TV saving that jerk's life. How's the tooth?'

'All fixed.'

Passang flashed a smile, showing his new crown. The guides gathered round, laughing and ribbing him about Malcolm Buttworth, about the tooth, about his star appearance on television.

Andrea drove the bus up to the glacier. The tourists were split into two groups of six so that each group had at least two guides. She took one group into the carpark with Passang for a safety talk, and Bernard, Hans and Gunter took the other six to a large information sign for their safety talk. The two groups came back together, and Andrea led everyone on the track up to the ice. She wore a wide-brimmed leather hat leaving her ears uncovered. When they arrived at the ice, she listened for rocks, water, cracking ice: any indication of a safety risk to their charges for the day.

On the glacier, the two groups split once more. Bernard walked ahead with his group of tourists and guides. Andrea led her group, with Passang following close behind her. She stopped occasionally to survey the ice, reading the signs for hidden crevasses, and scouting for holes. Passang pointed out secure routes to the icefall and spotted ice caves and a pool of milky blue water surrounded by ice columns, photo opportunities for the tourists.

Bernard appeared on the ice face above Passang and Andrea. He hurled schist rocks into the pool, making loud splashing noises.

'What was that?' said one of the tourists in a Geordie accent.

'It's Bernard. Must be a boy thing,' said Andrea, and led the tourists to the next sight, a blue ice cave.

As the end of the tour drew near, the separate groups headed by Bernard and Andrea converged at the foot of the icefall and crossed behind a large schist boulder the size of an armoured tank. Bernard held his ice axe in one hand as he approached Andrea. The sharp metal ends were the same browny orange colour as the old algae-covered rocks in the valley. She edged past him.

'You've got mushrooms,' she said, eyeing the pick.

Passang laughed behind her, the group of six tourists following in a line behind him. Bernard's eyes changed from blue to dark grey.

'If I put this axe into your head it wouldn't make any difference,' he said, looking at Passang.

'Sherpa skull is pretty strong,' said Passang.

Everyone laughed, except Andrea, who looked uncomfortable.

The Geordie tourist asked Passang, 'Is that her boyfriend?'

'Yep. Boyfriend and girlfriend.'

A grey cloud lifted off the ice as they walked down the glacier. Bernard's voice stuttered on Andrea's walkie-talkie.

'Where's Daddy Sherpa?'

'He's here with me,' said Andrea.

There was silence on the other end.

In the boot room that evening, the tourists removed their packs, raincoats, rain pants, socks and boots and left them in wet piles in blue plastic bins. Their faces were bright and energised as they thanked the guides and trickled out of the building into a dim evening. Passang helped Andrea put socks into the washing machine and hang boots up on the racks.

'We should go to the pub tonight,' she said.

'Yes, we toast the Sherpa hero,' said Hans in his thick German accent.

Gunter, his countryman, agreed with him, and they spoke emphatic German to each other.

'Yeah, let's go and watch the game,' said Passang.

Bernard emerged from the office with a cordless phone.

'TV3 again,' he said, handing the phone to Passang.

It was a producer from the newsroom. The taxi camera footage had gone viral.

'We'd like to interview you,' she said.

'What for?'

'People are interested in how a Nepalese Sherpa feels about saving the life of a drunken racist ranter.'

'Oh?'

All Black supporters filled the pub, with a few Springbok followers huddled in small groups. The Geordie tourist sat hunched over a large glass of beer. Black bunting and silver fern All Black flags dangled over the bar, and large New Zealand flags hung on either side of the television. The crowd applauded Passang as he entered the room.

Andrea took Passang's arm and they were ushered, with Bernard, Hans and Gunter, to a table laden with handles of beer. People shook Passang's hand.

One old man grabbed his shoulder and said, 'That bloody Invercargill bastard made me ashamed to be a Kiwi the way he talked to that taxi driver bloke. Not like you, mate. You are a top-shelf Kiwi Sherpa.'

'Ah, it was nothing,' said Passang.

When the All Blacks scored the match-winning try, Passang jumped up and punched the air. Andrea jumped with him, and then placed her hands on his chest and kissed him. He guessed she'd acted out of impulse in the heat of the moment. But her eyes had lingered on him far too long, and Bernard was watching them. Passang turned away from her and walked to the bar.

He could see Bernard and Andrea locked in stern conversation. Hans joined him at the bar, shaking his head.

'They arguing over there,' said Hans.

'I'm going home,' said Passang.

'Me too,' said Hans.

As Hans and Passang walked through the car park, Bernard ran out, grabbed Passang by the shoulder and spun him around.

'Hey, what are you doing?' said Passang.

Bernard jutted his chin out and shouted at Passang. 'You don't know what she's like.'

'I wasn't doing anything with your missus,' said Passang.

Bernard punched him in the face.

Passang's head jerked backwards. The new crown flew out of his mouth. He stumbled against a car door and collapsed onto the gravel. As he lay on the ground he saw people spilling down the steps from the pub. Andrea ran to his side and helped him up.

'My tooth,' he said, holding his mouth.

Andrea scrabbled about in the gravel and found the white ceramic crown.

'Come with me, Sherpa,' she said, holding his arm.

Passang tried to bat her away, but she fussed over him.

'You're hurt,' she said, watching Hans shuffling Bernard to the office.

Passang sat at the kitchen table in Andrea's flat holding his jaw.

'Does it hurt much?' she asked.

'Just a bit bruised. I'll have to go back to the dentist,' he said, moving his jaw from side to side.

'This will help,' she said, dabbing arnica on his bruised face.

He winced in pain. 'Look, I don't want to get in between you and Bernard.'

'We broke up while you were away in Queenstown. We've been growing apart for a while.'

'I didn't know.'

'Bernard didn't want to tell anyone.'

'So why did he punch me?'

Andrea put her hand on Passang's leg. 'If we didn't tell anyone then I guess he could pretend we weren't breaking up.'

'Why did you kiss me?' he said.

'Why do you think?' she said, laughing.

'I love my job, Andrea. He could fire me.'

'His father does all the hiring and firing. He won't fire you, his best guide, his famous Sherpa.'

'I better go home.'

'Don't go,' she said, and kissed him again.

The next day at Blue Glacier Tours, the guides scattered into various corners of the building. Bernard burrowed himself away in the office. Passang hid in the back of the boot room with Hans and Gunter, nursing a large purple bruise on his cheek.

'That's ugly,' said Hans.

'What happened to them while I was in Queenstown?' said Passang, trying to hide his broken tooth.

'What do you mean?' said Hans.

'She told me they broke up.'

'Not as far as I know.'

Tourists arriving for the first booking forced Bernard out of the office. He mumbled a grudging apology to Passang, offered to pay for the crown and blamed the drink. Over the next few days the pressure between them settled down. But Passang dreaded the close confines of the boot room gatherings, and was relieved to get away into Queenstown to visit the dentist. On his return, he kept to himself.

'Why are you avoiding me?' Andrea asked him.
'Why did you lie to me about breaking up with Bernard?' he asked in return.
'I didn't lie.'
'Don't you know Sherpas mate for life?' he said, half joking, but half not.

Despite his better judgment, he began to look forward to Andrea's banter. He noticed a shift around the region of his heart, some movement inside, although he didn't want to lose control. He saw her whispering in the office with Bernard and tried to put it out of his head, but it was all wrong.

With the continuous effort of trying to rein in his emotions, he'd forgotten about the incident with Malcolm Buttworth. Then one day after a tour when the tourists were leaving the boot room, saying their goodbyes and taking photos and buying souvenirs, Passang looked up from a bin of jackets and saw a man with shaggy red hair.

'Are you Passang Phurba?'
'Yep, that's me.'
'I'm Malcolm Buttworth.'
He'd lost weight. His face looked haggard, and there were dark rings under his eyes.
'I didn't recognise you,' said Passang.
'I'm sober now.'

'I won't invite you for a beer at the pub then,' said Passang, laughing.

Malcolm glanced around the room. Gunter averted his eyes. Bernard stood at the counter in front of the boot racks, sucking in his cheeks. Andrea and Hans sorted socks in the corner.

'How's your chest?'

'I still have more surgery to go. I just wanted to say thank you,' said Malcolm.

He looked uneasily at the other guides in the room and then looked down at his feet, rocking from side to side.

'I've been hounded by everyone. We've lost business. I tried to apologise to Mr Dareshak. But he won't talk to me.'

'Well, we all make mistakes we're ashamed of,' said Passang.

He looked over at Bernard, who was leaning on his forearms on the counter and peering up from under his hair. Passang turned back to Malcolm and placed a hand on his arm. Malcom flinched.

'Let's go next door and have a cup of tea,' said Passang.

'Sure,' said Malcolm, arranging his arm on Passang's shoulders.

A camera flashed somewhere, and Passang felt the weight of Malcom's arm lift off his body.

'Look. I just I wanted to thank you. I have to go now,' said Malcom.

He shuffled out of the boot room and into the waning evening light.

'Good riddance,' said Andrea.

'At least he's sorry,' said Bernard, glaring at her.

'Only because he got caught,' she said.

Passang followed Malcolm into the car park to a white four-wheel-drive truck with 'Helico Hydraulics' in gold lettering on the side. The lights switched on one by one in the pub next door. Malcolm heaved himself into the cab of the truck and wound the window down to look at Passang. Another man appeared from the direction of the boot room and climbed into the other side of the truck.

'Got the pics, boss?' said Malcolm.

'Yep,' said the man.

'Where are you heading?' said Passang.

'Back to Queenstown.'

'Take care on those roads.'

Passang waved farewell as Malcolm started the engine. Malcolm did not return the wave.

'Bloody bungas. They're even here in the snow.'

Malcolm's words reverberated in Passang's ears as he drove away. Andrea walked up to Passang in the car park as the light went out of the sky. He stared after the speeding truck. She cuddled into him and pulled her jacket tight.

'It's so cold tonight,' she said.

Passang kissed Andrea's head.

A quiet misty rain was falling, smudging the edges of the streetlights. He put his arm around her and led her back to the office.

'I don't know how you could even speak to him. I'm not surprised Bilal refuses to have anything to do with him,' she said.

Passang hadn't seen Bilal since they'd appeared together on TV3 News. He'd rung him a few times to check how he was though. Bilal had stopped driving taxis. The anxiety attacks were too much for him. He'd found a new job working from home analysing online surveys for a research company.

'Bernard wants the fuel taken up to the helipad tonight,' said Andrea.

'I'll run it up now,' said Passang.

'Thanks. See you when you get back, Sherpa.'

Andrea handed him the truck keys and ran into the boot room. He pulled the hood of his jacket over his head as he walked to the truck. On the glacier tour that morning he'd decided that he wouldn't carry on the charade with her any more. But he knew he might feel differently in the morning.

He fumbled with the keys, and dropped them on the icy gravel. As he bent over to pick them up a light came on in the office. Must be Bernard working late with the books, he thought. He drove to the petrol bowser and filled three cans. When he drove back past the car park, he glanced at the Blue Glacier Tours building. Two people stood silhouetted in the office window. They merged into an embrace.

Passang drove out towards the helipad. He had his foot on the accelerator, and was too distracted to feel the slight tug of the back wheels beginning to slide out as he drove around a gentle curve in the road. When the truck started to spin he realised he was on black ice, and overcorrected the steering wheel. The vehicle swerved out of control. He tried to right the wheels, wrestle them back in line, but it was too late.

The truck flipped over into a ditch and smashed into a tree, exploding in a ball of fire.

The rain fell softly on the people running from the pub, from the restaurant, from the store, from the motel, from the car park, from the boot room, from the office.

0.001

Niki heard her phone singing Lauryn Hill's take on Roberta Flack's 'Killing me Softly'. Why had she programmed such a doleful ringtone? The song lyrics echoed plangently, buried under sheaves of music. With great care, Niki replaced the woad-tinted Stratocaster into its black stand. Her long hands padded over the table in quick fluttering movements. Piles of paper and several books spilled onto the floor: *Blavatsky's Shamballah in the Gobi Desert*, *Gulliver's Travels* and *Orion Shall Rise*. At the final bar of the ringtone she moved a set list to one side and unearthed the slim red device. The caller's name appeared on the screen: Consuelo, her Argentine with the black hair and fiery green eyes. These interruptions made her so angry. She slid the green bar to answer.

'Hola.'

Consuelo breathed down the fibre optic cable and into Niki's ear. 'I can't go to Metallica tomorrow.'

Thrumming her fingers on the set list, Niki decided the first song was too slow. The first set tonight had to start with something more upbeat. She picked at a loose button on a formal black waistcoat hanging from the back of her chair. The old cat tunnelled his way through a plastic flap in the door and, standing regal as a statue, held a moment of yellow eye contact with Niki from across the room, before sauntering off. Niki followed the cat's progress into the kitchen. Glittering on the fridge door were the two prized tickets. Tickets she'd obtained through her cousin at great expense. This cancelling-out shtick that Consuelo always pulled was tiresome, unacceptable. She was unreliable. Niki exhaled.

'Fine. I'll take Cathy.'

'¿Qué? If you take Cathy, I'll never speak to you again,' said Consuelo.

Then she started with the shrieking. Not this again, thought Niki.

'No vayas al concierto con esa puta!'

Niki shook her head. It was laughable. She held the phone out and tapped the speaker function to save her eardrums. Consuelo's high-pitched tirade pierced the room. The cat raised his head from a silver food bowl, his tail curling into a question mark. Niki clicked her fingers and patted her knee, urging the cat to her side. But the old cat had heard this before. He would have none of it, and scampered back out through the cat flap. Niki laid the phone onto a heaped pile of chord sheets. 'Nothing Else Matters' peeked out from one side. How appropriate, she thought. She took the Strat from its tripod and began strumming to Consuelo's angry libretto.

'Are you there? Vete a la mierda!'

A thread of rainbow light pulsated on the floorboards as herds of towering white cumulus raced across the sun, jostling for a place in a pale blue sky. Niki leaned back into the lumbar support of her black office chair, raised her bare feet onto a leather ottoman and continued playing the Strat. When would Consuelo stop and take a breath? The Argentine was too much, too high-maintenance. There was no let-up. She picked up the phone and broke into Consuelo's rant.

'Consuelo, don't tell me you're going to the concert and then cancel. I'm taking Cathy, okay? I've had it with you.'

Bent-over willow branches in the garden waved their leaves in agreement, together with the sword heads of the tī kōuka trees. A sunburst clock tick-tick-ticked in the sudden void. Then Consuelo started again, with a vengeance. Niki drew a breath, and shouted at the phone. 'I'm hanging up, Consuelo. Goodbye!'

She dragged the red bar across the screen until Consuelo's voice was gone, and threw the phone. It skimmed along the surface of the pages, hit the wall, bounced back into a pile of notes, scattering them in paper waves, and disappeared. Niki sank into her chair. Women! She felt breathless, and reached for an inhaler in the waistcoat pocket. When would she ever meet someone suitable?

Niki walked into the student bar at 6 p.m. wearing a fitted suit and white shirt. Her short black hair was swept up into a lopsided quiff. Wolfgang, her cousin, stood untangling a microphone chord as she arrived. He looked up and waved at her from the stage. The other half of their duo, The Ellice Islands, he looked mesomorphic next to her lean frame.

'Hey, funny foot,' said Niki.

'Niulakita! Looking sharp.'

'Thanks.'

'How's the Argentine?'

'She's going nuts.'

Wolfgang slapped his forehead in mock grief. He laughed and checked another microphone.

'You need to settle down with a Tuvaluan girl, Nik.'

'What, like you have? I'm not cut out for it, Wolf.'

Niki waved at Charlotte, the sound technician, who manipulated the levels from a mixing desk at the back of the room. Her hair was spiked into a Mohawk, and she wore army camouflage jeans and a punk ripped T-shirt. A few students sat in the fading light drinking beer and talking in quiet tones. Niki unpacked her guitar. The stage sat low to the ground and looked small and cosy, like an illegal hermit shelter on a public beach. The stage, her safe place. Her head would not be far above those in the crowd, and she was tall enough to touch the ceiling. She felt like a giant in a dark religious grotto. She plugged the guitar into an amp on stage and played a few gloomy chords. Wolfgang tapped the microphone heads and popped his lips.

'Check, check, legal fees, legal fees, one, two.'

Niki played the first few bars of 'Nothing Else Matters', her favourite song. They changed, her favourite songs, like the women in her life. She wished they wouldn't change: the women, that is. One of the drinking students clapped, raising a host of dust particles into the afternoon light. Charlotte gave the thumbs-up from the mixing table. Several other musicians arrived. They drank from dark green bottles of beer and chatted with Niki and Wolfgang. Niki stepped off the stage to let the other musicians set up their instruments. She sat down in a square alcove to hone the tuning on the Strat before placing it back into its case for the evening performance. Wolfgang had arranged this gig, an island fundraiser. Something to do with a de-salinisation plant on Funafuti. He sat down on the bench sofa opposite her, placed two glasses on the low table and poured beer into them from a large jug.

'You need to find someone to take back to the islands,' he said.

0.001

'I'm not going back there. There's no future for me in Tuvalu. There's no future for anybody there.'

Niki had had this conversation over and over again with Wolfgang. He shook his head and laughed.

'Come back with us next month. It'll be easy. A holiday in the sun,' he said.

'More like free labour for your de-salinisation project. I have books to read, Wolfgang. And besides, no women in Tuvalu would go for me.'

Niki watched Charlotte talking to a tall thin student as she checked the fold-back monitors at the front of the stage. Charlotte pointed the student's attention over towards Niki and Wolfgang. Niki wondered how he knew Charlotte. His hair was dark and curly and fell to his shoulders, and his expensive-looking glasses caught the late sun as he talked to Charlotte with a bowed head. Charlotte took him to Niki and Wolfgang's table.

'Hey Charlie,' said Wolfgang.

'Hey Wolfgang – this is my friend Harold. He's a scientist. He wants to talk to you about Tuvalu.'

'Talofa. This is my cousin Niki,' said Wolfgang.

'Hello.' Niki shook Harold's hand.

It felt clammy, and she drew her hand back quickly and wiped it on her sleeve. Gross, student bacteria, she thought.

'Can I offer you a beer?' said Wolfgang.

'Um ... no thanks. I don't drink,' said Harold.

Wolfgang and Niki glanced at each other. Harold shifted his feet and folded his arms. He looked at Wolfgang and said, 'Charlotte told me you're from Funafuti.'

'Yeah, he's royalty,' said Niki.

Wolfgang puffed his chest out and said, 'My brother is High Commissioner for Tuvalu at the United Nations in New York.'

'Is that right? I'm going to Funafuti next week to collect data on sea levels,' said Harold.

'You should talk to my brother. He's hot on this climate change stuff. He went to the conference in Paris.'

'Tuvalu did great at the Paris conference, and the one in Copenhagen,' said Harold, his eyes opening wide.

'But how much time is there before we sink into the ocean?' said Wolfgang.

'We haven't collected enough longitudinal data to make a prediction with any accuracy,' said Harold.

'So we don't need to abandon ship yet?' said Niki.

'You don't need to abandon ship at all. The engineering options are incredible. Have you heard about the oil rig cities?' said Harold, straightening the glasses on the bridge of his nose.

'Pardon?' said Niki.

'The oil rig cities. Floating cities, like oil rigs, but cities. Your government is looking at building something along these lines if Tuvalu sinks any further into the sea,' said Harold, blinking fast, as if he had something in his eye.

'What, like Laputa?' said Niki.

'More like Deepwater Horizon,' said Wolfgang, smirking.

'Well, it's more likely they would use pneumatics and indirect displacement to rest platforms on trapped air,' said Harold.

What a nerd, thought Niki. She excused herself and went to the bar to get more beer. The phone started singing its mournful tune in her pocket. She must change her ringtone. Consuelo again. Niki didn't feel up to another argument here in the bar. She cancelled the call and pressed the mute function. She could see Wolfgang and Harold deep in conversation in the distance. She decided to ring Cathy to make sure she could go to the concert with her tomorrow night.

0.001

Wolfgang wouldn't go with her. He didn't like heavy metal. Damn the Argentine. She went back to the table with another jug of beer.

'Hey Niki. This guy is smart,' said Wolfgang.

Harold blushed. What man blushes like a girl? thought Niki.

'Tell her what you do,' said Wolfgang.

'I'm an atmospheric physicist. I suppose you could call me a climate scientist,' said Harold.

Niki stifled a yawn. A total atmospheric bore, she thought.

'My primary research field is the physics of glaciers, waves and sea circulation. I'm researching the effect of retreating glaciers and ice caps on rising sea levels. Most of the time I collect and analyse data from tidal gauges on Tuvalu. A land mass version of the canary in the coal mine.'

Wolfgang scratched his chin. 'The canary in the coal mine, huh?'

'Well, *I* think so. I collaborate with a colleague based in Ilulissat, in Greenland. He works for the World Glacier Monitoring Service, and he collects data on the Jakobshavn Glacier. Glaciers act as canaries in the climate change mine,' said Harold.

Niki stared at him. Wolfgang laughed.

'Glaciers and Tuvalu, canaries. This is poetic. I haven't seen a glacier in the flesh, or a canary,' said Wolfgang.

'They are phenomenal – glaciers that is – and canaries too, beautiful birds. The calving front of Jakobshavn is five kilometres wide. Moves nineteen metres a day and dumps thirty-five cubic kilometres of ice into the sea per year,' said Harold.

He talked fast and breathlessly, his words clipped, disjointed.

'No wonder we're sinking,' said Wolfgang.

'Greenland should do something with all that ice. They could ship it off to Saudi Arabia and make millions of dollars,' said Niki, smirking.

'They could ship it off to one of Aunty Vau's gin parties and get rid of it in one hit,' said Wolfgang.

Niki laughed at the thought of her aunt on her father's side. She pictured Aunty Vau dancing at Pasifika with the other aunties, her face shining black in the heat.

'You better be careful. Aunty Vau will give you a hiding if she finds out how cheeky you are behind her back,' said Niki.

Harold tittered uneasily. What a drip, thought Niki.

'Okay, Harold, analyse this. How many women would make a suitable girlfriend for me out of the four million people in New Zealand?' she said.

Harold looked dumbfounded.

'Leave the man alone. He's a scientist, not a dating service,' said Wolfgang.

Charlotte had joined the table now, and a few of the musicians looked on.

'I collect data about waves and I analyse changes in levels and interpret them and try to extrapolate into the future,' said Harold.

'If you can collect wave data and interpret it, you could do the same with women, couldn't you?' said Niki.

'Well ... it would depend on so many variables,' said Harold.

'Here are my variables, Harold. Dark hair, green eyes, feminine, smart, no mental health issues, no food issues, no alcohol issues, no drug issues. Simple.'

'You are describing the Argentine. You've already got her,' said Wolfgang.

'Not on the mental health issue at the moment,' said Niki.

The musicians sneered in the background. A group of students at a low table noisily debated the rules of a drinking game. Several jugs of beer huddled in the centre of their table, glinting orange in the filtered afternoon sunlight. The game was taking a while to get going. Two of the students turned their attention to Niki and Harold's conversation.

'Go on Harold. You can do it,' one of them shouted.

'But ...'

'And no fucking Tourette's!' said one of the students.

'Fuck no. I don't want any fucking Tourette's,' said Niki.

Charlotte snickered. Harold straightened his glasses on the bridge of his nose. 'Okay,' he said, pulling an iPad out of his bag. He typed onto the screen.

'Back of the envelope? Population of New Zealand four million. Lesbian, ten per cent of women: reduces the number to 200,000 straight off."

'No butches,' said Charlotte.

'Between thirty and forty years old?' said Harold, raising his eyebrows and looking around the gathered group, which had grown in numbers.

A wave of nodding heads swept the room.

'Hard to say, with any accuracy. My educated guess is 40,000.'

'Woohoo, gin party at Eden Park,' said Niki.

This raised a murmur from the group.

'Take the singles then subtract the unemployed, alcoholics and addicts and those living outside Auckland.'

'There won't be any left,' said Niki.

Harold crossed his legs and peered over the top of his glasses like an old professor.

'Go on. I'm kidding,' said Niki.

'Subtract blondes, redheads, blue eyes, brown eyes. Everything except black hair and green eyes, right?'

'Yep,' said Niki.

'No racists,' said Wolfgang.

'Okay, take out all the white women,' said Harold.

'No way! I love white women. Especially if they have black hair and green eyes,' said Niki.

She glanced over at the group of students playing the drinking game, who had now split into two groups. Those playing the game erupted into a frenzy, demanding that one of their number should scull a large glass of beer. Those who had abandoned the game sat listening to Harold.

'Okay, we'll subtract 90 per cent of white women?' said Harold.

'Fine, leave ten in there,' said Niki.

'The calculation is ten per cent, not ten people,' he said.

'And no fat chicks,' said Niki.

'Oh, now who's going to get in trouble with Aunty Vau?' said Wolfgang.

'No ugly chicks!' one of the students shouted.

'Look, you'd have an estimate, a probable percentage, of zero point zero, zero, zero, zero, zero one, or ten to the power of minus six,' said Harold.

'What does that mean?' said Niki.

'The number is minute. Think of a million but in reverse. Say you cut a chocolate cake in half and then in half and then in half again and again until you have a single crumb, and then cut the crumb in half a million times. The number ten is the chocolate cake and the number of times you cut it in half is represented by a zero. Ten to the power of minus six, it's called.'

'That's too many zeros for me. I'll just call it zero point zero zero one. So how many women is that?' said Niki.

'Four.'

Niki sat up in her chair. 'Wow, four women. Cool.'

Harold held up a hand. 'Wait. As in climatology, there are always other variables which must be taken into account.'

'Like what?' said Niki.

0.001

'Maybe a catastrophic event, such as a meteor strike pulverising Jakobshavn and releasing the whole glacier into the sea,' said Harold.

'And it sinks Tuvalu so we have to build oil rig cities,' said Niki.

'In this case, I would say there is at least one other person with the same variables as you who will be pursuing these same four women.'

'Looking at her!' said Charlotte, pointing her thumbs back at herself. She laughed and stood up, held her arms in the air and ran in a circle, making V salutes with her fingers.

'Statistically that means two for you and two for Charlotte,' said Harold.

This produced another round of victory arm waving from Charlotte.

'One is all I need. It's great to have a spare up my sleeve though,' said Niki.

Dying sunlight angled in lengthening shafts through large windows next to the stage. The students went back to their drinking game. They pointed at one man with their elbows, insisting he scull a large glass of beer. Charlotte wandered off to the mixing desk, still waving her arms in the air in victory salutes. The musicians continued unpacking their instruments and checking sound levels. Niki looked at her phone. She had missed several calls from Consuelo. She turned the ringer back on. Maybe she should call her. She could persuade her to go to the concert, play a game with her and bribe her somehow.

'Well, that was all very interesting. So have you been to Funafuti before?' said Wolfgang.

'Yep. This will be my second time,' said Harold.

Niki noticed a young woman walk into the bar at the end of the room. Her hair was spiky, short and black. She wore a black dress and Doc Martens. Her arms were chalk-white, and the sun shone into her eyes. Bright green eyes. Niki sat up straight. Wolfgang and

Harold stopped talking. The students fell silent. The woman walked over to Harold and kissed him on the cheek. Harold cast his eyes to the floor.

'Hey Harry,' said the woman.

Wolfgang's eyes widened, and a smile crept across his face as he turned to Harold and then to Niki.

'Aren't you going to introduce us, Harold?' he said.

'Oh. This is my sister Gemma,' said Harold.

Wolfgang laughed and held up a glass of beer in salute.

'And here comes your green-eyed beauty, Nik.'

Niki turned to see Consuelo walking into the bar. She jumped up and walked to greet her.

'I'm sorry,' said Niki.

'You didn't answer your phone. I've been trying to ring you all day,' said Consuelo, tears welling on the edges of her large green eyes.

Niki hugged Consuelo and led her to a seat in the corner of the room, glancing back at Wolfgang, who raised his glass again and laughed.

'I don't like the horrible crowds at those concerts,' said Consuelo.

'You'll be okay. We're not in the mosh pit. I booked good seats by the stage,' said Niki.

She draped her arm around Consuelo's shoulders. 'Have you heard of floating cities?' she said.

Consuelo shook her head, and her long black hair fell over Niki's arm.

Melt

Rena looked from the back seat of the factory truck towards Rangitoto Island glittering on the horizon. The giant volcanic cone sat hovering on a mirage layer of quivering blue as though skimming along the surface of the ocean. It looked like an alien space craft about to take off. Vivienne sat beside her, but Rena dared not say anything to her or even look in her direction. They both stared out of the windows as Manu Koula steered the truck across the northbound wing of the Newmarket overbridge towards SkyCity. His brother, Tommy Koula, rode shotgun. Their huge Afros filled the front cabin.

Rena heard the radio announcer say that Auckland had not recorded a temperature this high since 1872: it was a sweltering thirty-two degrees. Such high temperatures are normal in Rabi, Rena's first home. Her home was now in Howick, but her first home would always remain Rabi, and Marenanuka Tonganibeia would always remain Rabian. Kiwis struggled with the correct pronunciation of Rabi. Rena tried to explain the invisible M in front of the B: you said it 'Rambi'. But they didn't get it. One time for a laugh she had written 'Rabid' on a form that required her to state her ethnic origin. Although why ethnic origin held any importance for a Las Vegas ice sculpture competition remained a mystery to her. On your birth certificate or a census form, she could understand, but an ice sculpture competition in a desert city founded by gangsters? The Las Vegans had rejected her entry on the basis that she had entered a non-existent ethnicity. She had tried to point out to the organisers that Rabi was an actual country, a Pacific island.

'Those ignorant Las Vegans think I'm joking or something,' she said to Vivienne.

Vivienne had intervened on her behalf and explained to the organisers that in fact Rena was a New Zealander. After much to and fro the Las Vegans relented and let her into the competition. So began her famous partnership in ice sculpture with Vivienne. They carved intricate and complex pieces, and had won a gold medal at the Las Vegas competition with a rambling undersea fantasy, complete with Venus rising from the sea in a fluted scallop surrounded by her winged erote twins Himeros and Pothos and gigantic pearls inside enormous oysters, mermaids, whales, taniwha and the entire city of Atlantis.

Their partnership in life had begun much earlier, as children in the Polar Bear crèche in Auckland.

After the incident with the Las Vegans, Rena grappled for a while with giving herself an appropriate autonym; she had discussed it with Vivienne on many of their delivery runs.

'After all, would you call people from the Gobi Desert Gobid or Gobian?' said Rena.

'What about Gobits?' said Vivienne.

'No, then I would be a Rabit and Gobi children would be teased at school and called Hobbits. And Malian children would be called Malits,' said Rena.

'What if the Malits hit the Hobbits on the head?'

'Haha, so funny.'

'What about Raboid, or Rabo?'

'Nah, then I'd be called Rambo or Rainbow.'

'And Rabo is a Dutch bank,' said Vivienne.

'What about Raboi? Yes, we have it. I'm a Rainbow Raboi.'

'Rainbow Raboi it is. You can't call your people Rabis either. Such a name would be problematic for the vets and the Jews.'

Rena shared this joke with her Jewish doctor, Rachel Firestone, although Dr Firestone understood the dilemma and said, 'Meh. In Hebrew "he" means "she", "dog" means "fish", "rock" means "soft", "cuckoo" means "ponytail" and "mafia" means "bakery".'

To which Rena retorted, 'Well I've been to the mafia city, and it did strike me as half baked.'

In the end she settled for Rabian. Most people could not make out her racial or gender identity, and would construct it for her according to their own reality. One day a white woman having trouble being understood by a Saudi Arabian shopkeeper turned around to her and said, 'Young man, can you speak English?' Another time a tourist on the bus spoke to her in Spanish. Another time a small child at the beach ran up to her yelling 'Japanese man! Japanese man!' She would stare at these people in disbelief.

Those who knew the troubled history of Rena's home would debate whether she was truly Rabian at all. In fact Rena was of Banaban descent; her people came from the raised coral island of Banaba within the Gilbert Island chain, more accurately known as the Republic of Kiribati. The British had displaced the Banaban people to Rabi to suit their purposes, and in turn displaced the indigenous Fijian people who had been living on Rabi to the nearby garden island of Taveuni. In unguarded moments, so the Banaban story goes, the English were heard to whisper among themselves that they had used phosphate royalties from Banaba to purchase Rabi in order to resettle (that is to say, get rid of) the inconvenient Banabans so they could strip-mine Banaba of its remaining precious phosphate, in a carelessly circular process. Today this is well-known history, and still a topic of angry debate for Banabans and I-Kiribati and Fijians when they gather around the kava bowl. Of course, nobody in England remembers or even cares one jot about any of it, as you would expect. This is way too complicated to explain to a woman seated opposite you when you're speed dating and you only have three minutes to talk.

Rena had tried speed dating once with her ice queen, Vivienne. Vivienne wanted to go for a laugh. Rena went along, as she always did with Vivienne, because she had loved Vivienne from the first, since their childhood together running around in the Polar Bear crèche. They would often tiptoe past the ice room and Vivienne would squeeze Rena's brown face and hug her and then run away laughing and puffing white steam from her mouth, her shiny orange hair folding over and over as she looked back at Rena. She had no need to explain anything to Vivienne, and so when the circle changed and Vivienne sat across from her at speed dating, Rena said, 'I love you' straight off. Vivienne looked at Rena and said, 'I love you too.' And then she laughed, and they'd sat there for the next two minutes and fifty-eight seconds laughing and talking about ice, as they always did. Ice, the first love of Vivienne's life and the second love of Rena's life.

When Rena was very young, her parents had continued the displacement tradition and travelled to New Zealand looking for opportunity, settling in Howick. Her father had found work as a labourer at the Polar Bear Ice Factory, delivering party ice to supermarkets and petrol stations. The owner of the factory, Mr Watson, had started with block ice and then diversified into party ice. Out of a sense of loyalty to some of his customers (old-timers in historic Fencible cottages who hadn't made the change to refrigerators) he had continued delivering block ice to them for their ancient ice boxes. Rena's father would saw the ice blocks into slabs and carry them on his shoulders into refrigerated trucks. Other labourers at the factory also hailed from the tropics (Mr Tugia from Samoa, Mr Koula from Tonga and Mr Singh from Fiji), and they each had children, lots of children. Mr Watson, a staunch Catholic, had six young and boisterous daughters who ranged around the factory during the holidays like a flock of lambs. Rena joined the Watson flock, as did Fagaloa Tugia, Manu and Tommy Koula and Priya Singh. Having eleven children running around at holiday times meant the warehouse was more like a childcare centre than a centre of business. Mrs Watson came up with the idea of converting the unused storage room at the back of the warehouse into a holiday holding pen for the children, and the Polar Bear crèche came into being. The dusty room was cold and echoed. But Mr Watson swept and mopped the floors and the walls. He painted the room white and dragged in old signs saying 'Polar Bear Ice Factory' in elaborate lettering, and old cardboard figures of polar bears and snowmen, and fluffy toys with the stuffing coming out.

Rena and Vivienne would escape from the rest of the flock to watch their fathers in the ice room, cutting massive steaming ice blocks into cuboid lumps that they would slide into cardboard boxes and stack in the freezer. Sometimes Rena's father would stage a show for them, heating a fat nickel ball bearing with a blowtorch until it glowed red-hot. Using a mammoth wrench to pick up the glowing ball, he would place it on top of a cut-away block of ice. Rena and Vivienne would clap and laugh as the red-hot ball sizzled and melted its way right through the cracking hunk, water gurgling up behind it, over-flowing from the top and spurting out of fractures it left behind as it tunnelled its way to the gravelled floor. They would play with the left-over ice blocks wearing their father's old ice gloves, pushing the blocks about and smoothing them into shapes on the rough concrete. Even as young children they saw shapes in the blocks, and would compete with each other to see who could make them into the best dice, face, cat, igloo.

Inevitably, Rena and Vivienne melded into the Polar Bear work force. Many of the flock joined the business. The Koula brothers worked in the ice room and drove delivery trucks. One of them had his own courier company. Fagaloa Tugia burrowed his way into the Watson fold to become floor manager. Diane Watson went to university and became the accounts manager. Caroline Watson became the dispatch manager. As for Vivienne and Rena, Mr Watson made a strategic decision to capitalise on their talents, and diversified one arm of the business into ice sculpture: ice bars, ice glasses, party pieces, ice wedding cakes. Vivienne and Rena could sculpt whatever the customers ordered.

Sky City became their main customer, making continuous large orders of ice sculptures for medical conventions and trade fairs and fancy dinners for government dignitaries. The most recent order was for a large curved ice bar with corner features of ice dolphins and winged horses for the Nightclub and Alcohol Trade Fair, where it was rumoured there would be many Las Vegans in attendance.

Rena and Vivienne needed six days to make the sculptures. On the first day Rena half-filled the curved bins with water and left them in the freezer to solidify.

The next day, as Vivienne placed bottles onto the frozen slabs, she said to Rena, 'Fagaloa asked me to marry him.'

'What a fool!' said Rena, and she laughed.

Vivienne put down the bottle she was holding. 'Rena ... I said yes.'

'You're joking, right?'

'No, I'm not.'

'Well, you're an idiot. That's stupid. He should just fuck off.'

Rena ran from the freezer and didn't come back until the fourth day, when she returned through the loading bay. Fagaloa was standing on the dock, directing the load-up of a truck, officious with a clipboard. She ignored him and went straight to the ice room. The curved bins lay open in a line. Each one stood half full with frozen water. She could not see Vivienne anywhere, but it was clear that she had been working in the room. As planned, she had placed bottles of green and red top-shelf spirits in ordered rows on the flat layer of ice inside each curved bin. Rena straightened one or two bottles, her hand lingering on their smooth surfaces, before filling the bins to the top with water so as to submerge them. She left the cold ice room to do its freezing work, to grip the colourful bottles in icy suspension. Fagaloa had left the loading bay, and so had the truck.

The next day Rena returned to the ice room to start carving the corner piece dolphins and winged horses. She hesitated at the thick plastic vertical blinds hanging across the entrance to the cold room. Vivienne's figure moved in ghosted profile behind them. Rena put on her waxed ice coat and gloves and drew the hood up over her head. Shuffling into the ice room sideways like a crab, in bulky boots, with a toolbox in one hand, she looked over at Vivienne in red gloves and a puffy green coat, busy carving outlines onto new slabs of ice. They didn't talk, merely worked. Rena blocked out the shapes around Vivienne's grooved outlines with a small orange chainsaw, the noise loud enough to drown out any hope of talk. They carved for hours, until the dolphins leapt higher than usual and the winged horses reared up in anger rather than trotting in orderly ranks. But by the time it came to polishing and finessing the sculptures, the ice animals appeared calmer. Rena and Vivienne melted the dolphin noses into shape with tiny blowtorches and smoothed them to a clear shiny finish with heated spatulas. They chiselled the horse wings into light feathers.

Fagaloa poked his head through the plastic blinds as Rena sat putting her tools away. He hovered there as if decapitated and held in place on a pike staff, until the rest of his body slithered vertically into the room. He looked at Rena for a second and looked away. She ignored him. Vivienne hunched over her work, smoothing the curves of a dolphin's icy tail. He squatted next to her and whispered something. She stood up angrily and left the room. Fagaloa shook his head and looked at Rena, who lifted her chin and stared at him as he stood and followed Vivienne. Rena finished packing away her tools and went into the moulding room to talk to the Koula brothers. They wore white overalls and white gumboots with full-length white ice coats, and hoods drawn up over their massive black Afros. She felt calm in their presence: they were like her brothers. They had an uncomplicated view of life. From the ice mould machine they had produced one thousand hexagonal ice glasses and packed them into cardboard boxes.

'How's the bar looking?' said Manu.

'Finished. We need to winch it out of the bins. How are the glasses?' said Rena.

'All done. We'll get the bar into the truck in the morning. You will be here, won't you?'

'Of course I'll be here. How's she going to install it without me?' said Rena.

Manu stared at her for a moment. He had always been there for her, since childhood. He looked at her with a strange tilt of his head.

'What?' she said.

'I know how you feel,' he said, his eyes soft.

'How could you possibly know?' she said, and walked out of the room towards the loading bay.

Her ice coat swung as she walked, shedding ice particles onto the ground behind her. Vivienne and Fagaloa gesticulated at the end of the dock in heated conversation. Rena ignored them. The hot loading bay oppressed her, and she walked quickly to get away from their sordid carry-on. She returned late the next morning to help load up the ice sculptures. Fagaloa and the Koula brothers had winched the bar blocks onto pallets, and were leaning into them trying to slide them into the refrigerated delivery truck. Vivienne stood watching and fanning herself in the heat of the loading bay. She had piled her hair in orange layers on top of her head. Her shirt was open at the neck, and she held a melting piece of ice to her clavicle. Her eyes looked fluorescent pink, as if she had been crying. She saw Rena, and came over.

'Rena ... I ...'

The heat on the loading dock felt unbearable. Rena pointed with her eyes at the pallet loaded on to the truck. The edges of the cardboard boxes had begun to crinkle as melt water seeped through.

The traffic had come to a complete standstill half an hour ago. Rena cast her eyes over the cursed incline of Mount Hobson, with its tennis courts of heated pitch surfaces. Nothing moved except the shimmering heat waves coming off the roofs of the air-conditioned homes below. Vivienne turned to look out the window, red and green light from the dashboard reflecting onto the curve of her cheeks. Rena wanted to apologise, but not here in the truck. Tommy and Manu Koula sat in the front of the cabin with their round Afros filling the roof and their muscled brown arms resting on the door frames. Manu tied a bright red bandana around his head, pulling his hair into a tall tube. The RT radio chirruped and beeped as Tommy spoke into the mouthpiece.

'We're stuck on the overpass,' he said.

Caroline Watson's voice echoed through the tinny RT box and into the corners of the truck cabin.

'Truck and trailer jackknife at the Khyber Pass off-ramp. How's the diesel?'

'Should be okay,' said Tommy.

Rena sat quiet, listening to the idling engine, the hum of the air conditioning fan pushing cool air around her face. She could hear the rhythmic beat of the motor, and thought about the ice in the back. She turned to Vivienne.

'You're pregnant, aren't you?' she said.

Tommy looked at her in the rear vision mirror, his eyebrows raised. Vivienne's eyes brimmed with tears.

'We might as well turn the engine off. It'll run out if we leave it going, and then we'll be stuck here,' said Rena.

'We can't turn off the engine; the ice will melt,' said Vivienne.

'What the hell do you care?' said Rena, and she opened the passenger door and jumped onto the sticky asphalt bridge.

As she exited the truck a blast of hot air enveloped her, and she gasped at the shock of heat. Traffic packed the bridge, bumper to bumper. People climbed out of their cars and strained their necks above their rooftops to see what had happened ahead of them on the bridge. A Sikh taxi driver leaned against his car in the next lane, a white dastar, white beard and handlebar moustache lending him an air of nobility. He nodded at Rena.

'This isn't going anywhere,' he said.

Rena looked at him and was about to say something when Manu appeared at her side.

'Wow, she's hot out here. What a pile-up,' he said.

Rena sighed.

'We don't have enough fuel to run the truck for hours.'

'Well, the bar will be a goner then, and the glasses,' said Manu. He looked down at his feet in their white gumboots. 'Look, I think it's a stupid idea for them to get married. But you know what the boss is like.'

'What? Catholic?' said Rena.

'I know it's crazy. But she's stuck.'

'No she's not. It's fucked and Vivienne knows it. So does Fagaloa, the drip.'

Manu shook his head and laughed. They leaned against the blue logo on the side of the truck, a polar bear on an iceberg bobbing in a beryl sea of melting ice cubes. A baby cried in an old Peugeot behind the truck. Steam hissed from under the hood of the car. The driver, a Nigerian man, had turned off the engine and stood looking at the mist-shrouded bonnet with concern while talking in rapid Igbo to a woman in the front seat of the car holding the baby.

'I'd be careful opening that hood. The radiator could blow,' said Rena.

'Oh, this is not good,' said the man.

Four children in the back of the Peugeot peered out of the window at Rena. She smiled at them and waved. Their mother looked worried as she sat in the front seat holding the crying baby. Manu ambled over to the man, who greeted him in Igbo. Rena walked around the truck into the shade, and there was Vivienne leaning on the bridge railing. They stared at each other.

'It was just once. I was curious,' said Vivienne.

'Why do you have to marry him?' said Rena.

'Because he asked me.'

'Because he asked you! If he asked you to jump off this bridge would you do that too?'

'We're not kids any more, Rena. Don't try to mould me.'

'You told me you loved me.'

They stood silent, listening to the baby whimpering. Rena climbed onto the ladder and unlocked the back door of the truck. Vivienne didn't try to stop her. The truck doors swung open over the bonnet of the Peugeot and a cloud of ice fog poured out of the truck door onto the overheated car. Rena climbed into the back of the truck.

'What are you doing?' said Vivienne.

Rena disappeared into the wispy darkness and came back with a box of hexagonal ice glasses. She opened the box and handed it to Vivienne.

'We should hand these out,' she said, pointing to the Nigerian family.

Vivienne looked at her for a moment, her hands trembling. Rena jumped onto the road and carried the box of ice glasses to the Nigerian woman in the front seat of the Peugeot. She handed her one of the icy receptacles. The woman took the freezing glass from Rena and held the cold ice to her cheek, thanking her and jiggling the baby. Rena touched the baby's hand, and his little fingers closed around her forefinger. The baby laughed and Rena drew back in surprise, and then laughed along with him and his mother. She handed ice glasses to the children in the back seat, who squealed in surprise when they took hold of the cold objects. They talked in animated Igbo and laughed and drank from the ice glasses already melted full of water.

Rena turned to see a trail of melt water leading to Vivienne as she walked along the line of traffic handing ice glasses to frazzled people in their heated cars. She looked to Rangitoto, floating suspended upside down above the horizon in Fata Morgana mirage as if a ship could pass underneath. She walked back to the truck and opened another box of ice glasses. She looked back along the line of cars and saw Vivienne shining in distant heat waves at the limit of the vaulted highway, turning and weaving her way back to her.

Acknowledgements

Vinaka vaka levu to the editors of *Takahē* 70, where 'Glacier' previously appeared, and to the editors of *JAAM* 33, where 'Black Ice' previously appeared.

Vinaka vaka levu to the wonderful team at Huia Publishers – Eboni, Pania, Bryony, Jd and Te Kani – and to Daisy Coles.

Vinaka vaka levu to Selina Tusitala Marsh for her unstinting support, generosity and inspiration; to Lisa Samuels, Michele Leggott and John Newton for all their help and encouragement; to my first readers – the Hubcaps (Rosetta Allan, Andrene Low, Mary Nielson, Julie Ryan and Jan White), the MCW class of 2013 (Adam, Hannah, Katea, Krissy, Liz, Maddy, Mel, Tess, Tessa, Sara and Travis), Tulia Thompson and Theresa Koroi; to the late David Lyndon Brown for being such an inspiration; to Passang Phurba for a great day on the glacier; to Christina Jeffery for her help; to my sister Tagi Cole for all her support; and to Pamela Ford for all the love.